By the Light
of the Moon

An Anthology of
New Irish Fiction

Print Edition 2015

Licensed by Marble City Publishing

Copyright © 2015 the named authors

First published by Marble City Publishing in 2015

All rights reserved

ISBN 10 1-908943-52-1

ISBN 13 978-1-908943-52-1

FOREWORD

Long forgotten but dramatic events from history have inspired fourteen short stories in this collection of new fiction from Irish writers.

Drawn by the authors' imagination, these compelling stories reignite familiar historical themes once told through the satire of popular verse. Reinterpreted as an anthology, some tales are retold in their original setting while others are reimagined and adapted for today's world.

A glossary of all the associated rhymes and brief biographies for each author are included at the end of the book.

DEDICATION

In memory of Jane Avril de Montmorency-Wright

1936 – 2014

CONTENTS

THE ORANGES AND LEMONS EULOGY

BY R.A. BARNES

I can still hear the bells ringing, children's voices pealing out the rhyme. A hot summer's afternoon, just before the holidays. Those strange creatures, girls, turning cartwheels on the grass and squealing as the occasional glimpse of underwear was shared. Then joining the boys in a round of Oranges and Lemons, us sweating from our football game, them glowing from their gymnastics.

The innocence, breathless and without guile, boys and girls skipping through the archway of arms, smiles exchanged in the joy of the year end. Some of us would never see the other again, leaving for high schools on different sides of town. Others would eventually marry.

The horror as hands chopped down on damp necks in the finale, striking the heads from the unlucky last pair to pass through on the final verse.

We didn't know then what fate had in store. Brady the Gimp to be cut down by Motor Neurone Disease before he could marry. Bernie Dolan to finish his teenage life at the end of a rope in the local park. But we sensed the terror of fragile young lives. Well, I did.

Oranges and lemons, candy slices bought from Charlie Watkins' newsagent and sweet shop. Rows of glass jars standing to attention on wooden shelves, their contents sold loose by the quarter pound. Cough candy was my favourite. You preferred the sticky, sweeter stuff.

Old Charlie had something badly wrong with his skin. He was a wart-covered monster and we didn't want to buy sweets when he was behind the counter. We might catch his leprosy from a humbug. I often wondered if he was upset by us pretending to play outside, peering through the window until he had gone, leaving the less hideous Mrs Watkins to serve us.

We had our first taste of financial independence from the same lady. She took us both on as paper boys, in the days when milkmen delivered glass bottles. Daily news, gossip and nude girls appeared between pages of inky print. Michael the Midget was head paperboy and he managed us with dull efficiency and zero humour. I had the country delivery route called Box and spent an hour racing my bike between a few isolated farmhouses, enjoying the freedom. You took the dense and affluent Old Bedford Road on foot, built your muscles carrying the heavy bag of papers and raked in the tips at Christmas.

I was two years older and graduated to working in the petrol station next to our house, selling Embassy Gold cigarettes and Smurfs, filling unwitting foreign tourists' cars with the wrong fuel. My pay-packet outstripped yours but you still managed to save more. I've always been penny and pound foolish.

A year on and the menswear department of C&A was my new employer. I spent my Saturdays chasing leather jacket thieves, rearranging Crimplene trousers on their rails and measuring the inside legs of Pakistani gentlemen. Within a couple of months I bought my first guitar and discovered beer. A few months later I concluded that one or more of my drinking buddies were crooks and not buying their round of drinks. Friday, Saturday and Sunday nights out on the town always cost me a lot more than the other lads. As for you, even though we shared a room, I had forgotten you existed.

It would take until my second marriage for you to admit, during your best man's speech, that you had pilfered my pockets for change each morning that I lay comatose in my hangover bed. Over the course of time it was enough to buy that saxophone you wanted. Nobody could understand how you had saved so much. In later years you put down your confession as a joke. But we all heard you on the day.

Between those two marriages I found myself in financial straits. Live while you're alive was my motto and property problems found me with no rainy-day fund. You had made a few quid by that stage and stepped into the breach, insisting that I accept a loan of several thousand. This before I knew about the saxophone scam. I accepted both the money and a feeling of indebtedness. The younger brother had become an adult while the older was floundering in a pit of hedonism.

In honour of my own infidelity you explored your own mid-life crisis. But it was short-lived, once the financial implications became clear.

My sporadic lack of common sense seems to be inherited. I didn't lick it off the stones, as they say here. When our parents retired early they headed offshore – not to the Cayman Islands but aboard an overpriced thirty-foot catamaran during the Thatcherite boom. I was between homes and between wives, so you and yours became custodians of several of the seafarers' bits and pieces, including the cutlery set in its mahogany box with a piano finish. I think they meant to catch fish with a string and eat them raw, like Gollum. It didn't last, of course, and after three years of clothing and footwear rotting in the Essex coastal winters they retreated back on land, to Scotland which was about the only place they could afford to live. On request for return of the cutlery set your response, after spousal consultation, was 'Yours for twenty quid'. Presumably you didn't manage to insert all items in the orifice suggested by our mother.

I found my feet with that second marriage and my head rose above the financial mire. My offer to repay the loan was firmly rejected. You had come into some money and really didn't need any more. My need was doubtlessly greater than yours. I agreed, of course.

The benefits of a prudent life continued to accrue for you. Share options, company takeovers, property gains. When your wife demanded a brand new Audi you saw fit to bestow your old Ford on our parents who were struggling under the cosh of a small pension and the Scottish weather. 'It still doesn't make up for the cutlery set,' Mother confided in me.

Another decade passed and I received a call from our father. You had arranged to purchase their flat from the council, reducing their rent to a nominal amount and having the will altered to make clear your beneficial ownership of the property. Father was worried that I might think they were disinheriting me. I said I didn't need it. Mother promised to hide the antique plate collection from your wife and began to point out any items of value whenever I visited, which wasn't that often.

I made my own few feeble attempts at riches. Substantial share investments grew and vaporised with the fall of the Irish banks. A cashed-in pension dribbled away in the property crash. And I bought a few lottery tickets but none of those came up winners. Life hurtled towards its end in a harmless blur of mediocrity.

Now, at last, comes the chopper to chop off heads. I see your neck, pale and damp with the perspiration of hard-earned prosperity. Bells peal but the singing has stopped. The dance is done, knickers have been shown, the match is finished and our term is over. The last man's dead.

Your face is impassive. But wait. A single tear on your cheek as you look down upon my body in its silk-lined box. An American oak casket with brass handles. Good choice. Nothing but the best for me. I like the half-lid.

Farewell, brother.

SING A SONG OF SIXPENCE

BY MAURA BARRETT

I have a box of windfalls in the back of my car. Ralph gave them to me. I only know two Ralphs. The first is Ralph McTell, a singer/songwriter. Met him after a gig in the local hotel. I found him to be insightful and warm. I liked him because he was a storyteller. The second is Ralph Hogan, him of the apples. He is a whizz in the kitchen and I want to marry him. Unfortunately, that is not an option available to me. I knew another man once who did all of his own ironing of a Saturday afternoon, I wanted to marry him too. I am not in love with Ralph.

I had a friend once called Morrigan. She had raven hair and a heart of gold. She was beautiful in body, mind and spirit. She died by her own hand on All Souls' Day. They said it was her choice to make, that she had that right. That took a long time to reconcile. Sometimes that still jars inside my head. She was a vegetarian, wouldn't harm a fly. Since the day she was buried I keep seeing an old hooded crow. Sometimes she limps and other times she soars majestic, most times she sits aloft on a telephone wire near me, wizened, wise and mysterious. I've taken to chatting with the crow. No one else knows this.

I am a writer and a librarian. It's ironic: I spend all day presiding over books when really all I want is to be somewhere writing them. The public sector is a prison of sorts: there is the Pension Prison, the Permanent Position Prison, and the worst one of all is the Prison of Fear. I could just leave with my pen and paper, eke out words and stories; that's when Virginia Woolf's dictum goes around in my head. *A woman must have money and a room of her own if she is to write fiction.* So I write in the evenings and on weekends instead. Sometimes when I'm really in the grip of a story I will beat words out of keys deep into the night.

All Souls' Day fell on a Sunday this year. I woke early and tugged up the blind, wiped the condensation from the glass with an old rag and scanned the landscape. It was brighter than it should be that early in the morning. I scrambled back under the covers, knees tucked up beneath my chin, careful not to wake my husband. I wondered if I should ask him if I could give the whole day to writing. It wasn't that I needed his permission, I didn't, it just meant I had to commandeer his laptop and that might make him grumpy. He would also have to cook Sunday lunch, so it amounted to the same thing really. If I got up straight away, and left him to sleep on, I could get a few hours in. Then I could send him to the supermarket for pastry and I could bake apple tart and everyone would be happy. I'd make one for Ralph too. Not that he doesn't step up, it's just that's what I was thinking.

That's when it happened. A crow flew into the window pane. There was a thud and a raucous caw and a crunch splat sound. I got such a fright, the colour drained from my face and I shook. My husband just snored on. There wasn't even a shatter, just blood splats that drizzled down. I thought it even smelled fresh. That was it, a crimson stain framed in a pure white window, with sunny field systems beyond it and purple mountains beyond that again and a slither of blue sky.

I got up then, yanked on my denim jeans and a wool fleece against the cold. I didn't even shower. What was the point? What do you do when a crow dashes against your bedroom window and smears it with blood? Maybe it was a sign, and on the day that was in it too. I shivered again.

When I was little and lived with my Granny, one of the hens died. My cousin Antz and I buried her in a shoebox at the eastern edge of the tree grove. We made a cross out of ice-lolly sticks we'd been collecting to make baskets.

'Here lies Henny Penny. R.I.P.'

Then we had an argument. I was sure R.I.P. stood for 'Rest In Peace'. He swore blind it stood for 'Rise If Possible'. I didn't tell him then about the time I baptised him in the middle of the night, whilst he slept, with Holy Water, because he was a Protestant. I reserved that for our next row. Well it seemed Morrigan, morphed into a crow, had chosen today to end her crow life. So, little did it matter really if she rested in peace or rose if possible, it would've been nice if she'd been less tormented. Perhaps there was a shoebox in one of the children's rooms and perhaps I'd be able to prise it away without World War III.

Ralph knows about things, that apples have a lot of pectin for instance, especially crab apples. He is forever preserving things in jars: jams, chutneys, sauces. Then again librarians always do, they have to know everything, it's just part of the job, and if they don't know then they just know where to look to find out. What I admire most about him is how he has life in perspective. He is the king of the work-life balance.

If Ralph were here he'd say, 'Sit down there, Pet, you've had an awful auld shock.' And an iced gin and tonic would be landed in front of me.

Then he'd think in his own mind, 'Better go see if the blessed thing actually is dead. Otherwise we'll have an injured crow to contend with. She'll go straight into fixing things mode, as is her way. There'll be an expensive, futile vet visit because it would be beyond her to put the crow out of its misery.' He'd find a boulder and smash the crow's skull. Then he'd come in, wash his hands and help himself to a stiff gin and tonic.

The thing was that he wasn't here though. And Hubby was sound asleep. A well-deserved sleep at that. Did Virginia Woolf ever encounter this? I have a dishwasher, I have a washer/dryer, I have a ride-on lawnmower. When the children were babies I had disposable nappies and a steam steriliser. I drive my own car. I live in an age of equality and emancipation. She carved out her potential a whole generation before me, in times when women had even larger obstacles. Writing wasn't an option presently and it was all to do with that crow. Maybe I should have woken my husband. Fair play to Virginia Woolf.

Logic, when you are a writer and live in your head, sometimes refuses to prevail. I am a strong independent woman. Burying a crow before breakfast was a piece of cake. I even worked out that the part of the garden where the ashes went was probably the softest place to dig. I put on my Wellingtons, blue with buckles. I got them once for Electric Picnic. At the door, I dipped my fingers in the Holy Water font and blessed myself, that was habit.

Her left wing fluttered in the breeze where she lay on the recently steam-washed pavement to the left of the front porch. The indigo feathers squelching and oozing blood. My stomach heaved, I retched a bit. Then I went to the shed to get the shovel. Whiskers, the family cat, purred against my shin. I shook him aside, back towards his bed. Using the spade as a walking stick, I made towards Morrigan.

I could slide her onto the shovel in one swift lift if I got the angle right. It was then she sort of lurched forward a bit and croaked in pain. I screamed and dropped the shovel in a clatter, screamed again and bolted in a circle of insaneness. That was when Whiskers pounced and took off around the back of the house with the bird clenched between his jaws. I roared at the cat, cursed him, picked up the shovel and flung it in his direction. It clipped the tail light of my husband's car.

He found me jabbering on the back step.

'Whatever is the matter, precious?'

'I'm not making apple tart.'

THE FIDDLE

BY JEANNE BEARY

'That's a nice new car you have there, Scanlon. Although, I think you might have been driving a little bit fast.'

'Not a bit over sixty.'

I know this guy; there's no way he's wasting his lunchtime toting a speed gun. We're stopped at the side of the main northbound route out of the city. It's a normal, cloudy, dull day and the traffic is belting toward us and then braking erratically once the drivers see the squaddie. Nosy heads stare out the windows as the cars coast by. Out of habit, Jack fidgets in the seat beside me. He does this whenever we're being questioned. Today it's needless, we're carrying nothing. Through the space left by my rolled down window, the guard talks to me in a friendly fashion asking the regular questions. Where am I coming from? Where am I headed? Am I carrying anything illegal in my vehicle?

'This arsehole.' I tip my head towards Jack. The guard calmly ignores me as I try to get a rise out of him.

'So I see.' He inspects my motor again. 'It's a nice car alright,' he says calmly. 'How about you come down to the station and tell me where you got the readies to pay for it.'

I smile and look him in the eye. 'Not much to tell. I've got an auntie. She likes me if you know what I mean. I water her garden for her. She's very good to me. It was a gift. A thanks, like.'

'Yeah, he keeps her garden nice and wet alrigh'. Uses his hose he...'

The detective lowers his head as he interrupts, looking past me into the passenger seat.

'I wasn't asking you, Jack. I was asking Scanlon. I was just wondering how a lad with no job and a new baby just arrived, manages to get himself a set of wheels like this.'

The car is gleaming today. I polished it up last night for an hour. The child was screaming blue bleedin' murder and I needed to get the fuck out of the flat. Carina was walking back and forth wearing a track in the lino but the bab just kept on bawling.

'If you think this ride is nice, Garda, you should see the one he has at home.' Jack yowls at his joke and I jab him with my elbow.

'Shut up, you.'

He pants for a moment and then hoots again. I turn back to the guard.

'Like I told you, Garda, sir. It was a present from me auntie, for services rendered.'

'Yeah. A good servicing.' Jack keeps sniggering. He's always fucking laughing. It's this loud howl of hilarity until he runs out of air and starts panting and sniggering while he gets his breath back. Then, he howls again. The Garda rolls his eyes.

'Will that be all, Garda?'

He looks at us one more time as if hoping he'll miraculously get something on us. Then shakes his head.

'For now, Mr Scanlon.' He bends over once again to peer in at Jack. 'Goodbye to you too, Mr Russell. I hope ye won't give me any reason to meet up with ye soon.'

'Us? Of course not, Garda. Of course not.'

I let him pull away first, not wanting my roaring exhaust to give him an excuse to call us back.

I hear the baby half way down the street and think about turning around and heading away. The wad of fifties stashed away inside the flat keeps me going. The door has swollen with the recent rain and I put my shoulder to it and force it. It slams inward with a crash. Carina is still walking back and forth, the infant yelling in her ear.

'For fuck sake, Bren. I nearly had her asleep.'

'Yeah, it sounds like it,' I sneer.

'Well, are yous going to take her for a while, or wha'?'

'Or wha'.' I walk past.

'You're an awful prick,' she says.

I'm about to laugh but notice her tears. 'Look, I've got some stuff I gotta do. I promise I'll give yis a break later on, right?'

'Ye said that yesterday.' It's loaded with accusation, like it's my fault I have to make a few quid. 'I'm fit to collapse. Please.'

'Okay. Look, give her here for a few minutes and go take a rest. I can't stay long mind.'

She hands me the wailing bundle.

'Bren, next time you're out would you get me a bit of that stuff.'

'Wha'?'

'A bit of that white powder stuff.'

I look at her. 'What're ye talking about?'

'You know the stuff. The stuff ye can put on her gums when she's pushing teeth. It might make her stop crying. My head's about to fucking explode.'

'Ah yeah. That stuff. Right. Now, why don't you go on in, shut the door and lie down for a few.'

The door closes behind her. I walk back and forth gently shaking my screaming daughter until I hear the springs on the bed creaking. Then I look around for somewhere to dump the baby. She's already roaring; what harm can it do? I spot the pink bouncer under the table and tip the baby into it. I think about strapping her in, but those belts are always bleeding impossible to get right. It's not like she's going anywhere. She looks startled for a moment; not that she stops crying or anything but she appears surprised. I reach for the top drawer that holds the cutlery. Catching the knob, I pull the drawer from its runners as quietly as I can and place it on the floor beside the baby. Then I stick my hand in the cavity behind the

13

frame and fish around until I feel it. It's a box I keep to remind me of one of the first jobs I ever did. I open the latch. Nestled inside is one of the ugliest, most useless, not-silver, spoons you'd ever see in your life. Behind the felt-coated, spoon-shaped packaging are thick rolls of beautiful fifties. I peel off a few before slowly replacing the drawer.

The baby realises she's been dumped. The crying that I felt could get no worse has just become screeching with a new breed of intensity. Who knew something that small could be that fucking loud. I look at her bright red face, her squished up eyes and drawn lips. Jack says she's the spit of me but I sure as hell can't see it. She looks like a constipated piglet. I shrug and walk to the door.

I'm halfway down the street, still listening to the child, when I hear Carina shout.

'Scanlon, you're some fucking prick, you are.'

I lift a middle finger high above my head and keep walking.

'I don't know what you're moaning about,' Jack says later that afternoon. We're sat in our local, fondly known as 'The Cat', having a pint and doing a bit of watching. This is our turf so we like to keep an eye on incoming trade. 'She's a bleeding baby. Babies cry. She's living proof that you get it on with the fittest woman for miles around.'

'Probably more like got,' I mutter.

'What was that?'

'Nothing.'

'Like I was saying,' Jack continues, 'that baby's like a badge of honour. You share the scratcher with Carina Murphy. She was St Anthony's dish of the day, well, for as long as any of us lasted in the place. Quit moaning. You could be me.'

He had a point. Poor Jack. His gene pool must have been a manky shit-filled puddle. He's a small, wiry, pasty-skinned type of fella; whiskery, yet he wouldn't manage to grow a beard. Poor looks, but a big laugh, that's Jack for you.

'You could be going home to my heifer.'

I thought of his flabby girlfriend and her rolls of flesh and shuddered.

'But she's a really nice girl. She'd do anything for you.' I try.

'Yeah,' he looks at me and his voice is deadpan, 'and I've got a great sense of humour.'

Jack puts his hands out wide as if holding a washing machine and thrusts his pelvis back and forth a few times with a look of disgust on his face. Then he strokes the air lovingly in the shape of a neat hourglass and thrusts forward again this time looking ecstatic.

'I'm not saying anything,' he adds.

'Okay, you've made your point. I'd better go to the chemist. I need to repair a bit of damage.'

'Tell me you didn't hit her.' Jack sounds outraged.

'God, no; I just need to get back in the good books. She needs something for the baby. I'll meet you tomorrow for that other business.'

The pharmacy is clean and bright. Large strip lights shine down through carefully positioned slits in the ceiling. I shuffle towards the counter. Hooking a finger inside the collar of my t-shirt, I tug it, stretching the fabric. The saleslady, in her white coat, notices me and approaches.

'Can I help you?' she asks.

I cough. 'I'm looking for the white stuff.'

'I beg your pardon?' She sounds well-annoyed. 'Is this some type of joke?'

'No. No. I'm looking for the white stuff that makes gums numb.' She looks angry and appalled. I keep talking before she calls security. 'You know the stuff, for babies.'

'Ah,' her persona changes, she laughs and smiles, 'for babies.' She moves to a shelf on one side and picks out two boxes from the display.

'I have both of these,' she says, sticking the boxes in front of my eyes. She reads the text on one. 'Helps to ease the discomfort and pain associated with teething.'

Neither is familiar. Neither is expensive.

'I'll take them both,' I say.

When I get back to the flat, the baby is asleep. Carina turns away from me as I walk through the door.

'I brought you those packets.' I drop the boxes on the table.

'A bit late now,' she says. She heads to the room and shuts the door quietly behind her.

I open one of the cardboard boxes and pull out a little sachet. Tearing the corner I pour a little pile of flour-like powder into the palm of my hand. Using my other hand I dip a finger into the white dust and rub it on the gum above my teeth. I feel two things: one is a not unpleasant, fizzy, numbing sensation in my gum; the other is an idea forming in my brain. It'll keep until the morning. I climb in beside Carina but she's snoring gently.

'Can I get another thirty of these?' I say, holding up the sachet wrapper.

The assistant looks at me.

'They only come in boxes of twenty-four.'

'No, I meant thirty boxes.'

She reads the packaging warily. 'It's a natural homeopathic product. I can't see why not. I'll see what we have in stock.' She reappears carrying a pile of boxes and puts them through the scanner at the till.

I hand her money and she returns my change.

'Is it multiples?' she asks.

'Multiples?' I was crap at maths.

'Twins or triplets?'

'No. Just the one but she's teething like a bitch.'

'You and me only,' I stress. 'Not Carina, not the heifer,

not the mammy, no one else can know. If this gets out, it's bullets.' Jack is busy cutting, mixing a pile of expensive white powder with the contents of the thirty boxes I bought earlier. We're sitting in the shed at the end of his garden with the gear in front of us. I look at the back of Jack's house. His bird is upstairs. I can see her head bobbing up and down; her face appears and then disappears from view.

'What the fuck is she doing?'

He follows my gaze to see what I'm looking at.

'Her? She's getting fit.'

'What?'

'She's getting fit. She's on a little trampoline. Says she doesn't want to be called a fat cow anymore.'

'Are there people downstairs? Do they realise the danger?'

Jack just looks at me. He doesn't laugh. 'Yeah. Danny is.'

Like the devil when you mention his name, Danny, Jack's brother, appears. He's standing wobbling in the back doorway. He's clearly off his head. He sees us and waves. He shouts something.

'He looks fucked.' It's a stupidly obvious thing to say.

Unsteadily, his brother turns around and then drops his trousers, sticking his white sun-shy arse out towards us. Above him the girl keeps jumping, up and down, up and down. Danny then refastens his trousers, gives us the finger and staggers back inside. We watch unsurprised. For Danny Russell, this behaviour is fairly normal.

'Totally fucked,' Jack agrees. He looks down at the piles of white powder in front of him. 'Are you sure this stuff is safe?'

'Sure it is; they give it to babies for Chrissake.'

He shrugs and nods. We keep mixing and bagging.

We are cleaning up tonight. Down the lane near 'The Cat' we do a few sales. One client wants to check the merchandise. He rubs a trace on his gum. I wait and hold my breath. He nods, satisfied, another happy customer. We sell out. Our supply is gone. I pay the bossman. I don't trust Jack to carry it off. I shuffle towards him same as always and say the same things as always.

'Poor buyers … hard to shift … quiet night.'

He replies with the same reply as always.

'Scanlon, you owe me what you owe me.'

I drag out handing over the last bit, paying him in coins. Then he rolls up the window and drives away. Jack and I split our takings fifty-fifty. It was such a good night that the roll of notes barely fits behind the ladle. I'm just sliding the drawer back in when I hear her pad up behind me in her fluffy socks.

'That stuff is the business. She's sleeping again.'

'It sure is.' I agree. I smile at her. 'We should make the most of it.'

'I don't think so.'

When I join her later she rolls away. 'Don't you touch me.'

I don't. I fall asleep almost straight away. The baby crying wakes me. We lie in bed, Carina and I, playing a curious form of chicken. We are both awake and both pretending not to be. Eventually, I win. Her side of the mattress creaks as she stands to go tend to our daughter. I close my eyes and drift off again.

I feel like I've had the first decent sleep since the baby arrived. I open my eyes. It is definitely daytime but no cries have woken me. Maybe Carina took her out somewhere.

'Hey bud. Are you alright?'

I sit bolt upright and hear the howling laugh. I wait for the blood to reach my head and see Jack standing in the bedroom.

'What the hell are you doing in here?'

'The door to the flat was wide open. I was just

checking you were alright.'

'That's strange. Usually it's sticking.'

Nodding, I clamber out of bed and move to the kitchen. The drawer is on the floor. The box that held the ladle is open and empty; the plastic velvety lining is discarded to one side with a note saying, 'Goodbye, ye prick. I'm going somewhere you can't touch me.'

I growl and put my face in my hands.

But Jack, Jack just laughs, pants and then howls some more.

RESTORATION

BY ILONA BLUNDEN

Free at last from this murky darkness; into the light. I draw a breath of sorts, squint into an early autumn sun and feel its caress, the softest touch I have ever known, far removed from the last contact I felt on this earth. I know this place; it is familiar yet much changed. Shadows lengthen and I marvel at their trickery.

I have been in a stasis, a long, deep sleep, the weight of clay and rock pressing down on me. No light, no air, no space. Some were driven to find my resting place and for this I am grateful. Of course I helped them in their quest. The old maps still have their uses; no shifting plates moved ancient earthworks out of line.

I am revealed in all my glory, more naked than the day I first came into this world; a rebirth in this season of harvest. A little digging in the most unlikely place and you have been rewarded with a royal crop! When they first saw me lying there, they dared to believe it could be true. Architects of my release, hollowers of earth and stone, peered down at me, their faces filled with awe.

This season has not changed. I wake to those mutable colours of rust and cinnamon, copper and burgundy bursting forth, green-gold coins swaying in the breeze, merging and deepening in these days of light and air. Turning their rustic hues and I find I am still humbled by their beauty.

I see you leaning against red-brick dwellings and watching through wrought-iron gates. Metal carriages un-led by horse move of their own accord, swift and sleek they pass by. I am filled with a sense of wonder I have not felt since I was a boy. I have not seen this time before.

I hear the squawk of scavenger rooks as the full parliament observes me from its frenzied circuit. Swallows bank and wheel overhead, circling and returning, or do I imagine them? I miss the song of the lark in its morning reverie. This is no battlefield, no quiet meadow, no chapel of reflection.

Scrape and screech of metal on stone. The unholy noise of this beast! Its clang and roar and foul-smelling breath, and some other choking tarry fume, I know not what, yet this thing rescued me from my dark hell. Now and then, a faint yet constant hum or perhaps this is to be expected.

Earth turned, broken brick, sharp-toothed tile. I taste the chalk of my confinement and soil drying out, desiccated bone – my bones? I smell rose and lavender nearby or is that just my memory? Unfamiliar spices cause a pang of hunger that soon passes. Light-headed, I shrink back into my place of rest until I learn to breathe again. My parched throat catches and yearns to be quenched by life's sweet tang.

My cramped form stretches a little, not that you can see, crick-crack, an easing of sorts. I revel in this unexpected gift, the evening sun soothes my war-weary husk; I bask in it. I know it cannot always be this way, change has come and nothing will be still again for some time.

Like any man, I have regrets. None more so than the fate of those two young boys. They disappeared under my care and I cannot account for them. I shall let you be my judge; on this I can say no more. Once I would have given my greatest possession for rescue at my most pressing hour. It saddens me to see none of the kingdom's noble beasts in these surrounds.

The Lady in White scrapes away the mud and grit of ages, loosening its grip so I may be raised up and transported to a safe place. She holds me in her hands, all the while they tremble. I have already forgiven her the accidental crack upon my skull. What difference one more

21

wound? No matter now. I give myself to her and rest my unmoored head in her lap as I am taken to my new home. Out from the shadow of Greyfriars.

You think this some kind of coincidence? Something supernatural perhaps? Never underestimate the power I once had. If I desired to give the world irrefutable proof, it had to be now. My bloodline has all but died out, yet one or two still live. It is the right time and I made it so.

You may have thought me lost to the realm of myth but you may think again. I walked this earth, I lived and breathed, ate and slept, and fought to the end. An end so gruesome, it soon became a children's fireside tale.

It came fast for me, although I felt every blow. They did for me with a rondel dagger through the top of my pate. The reliable halberd sliced the back of my head more than once. Some kind of spear delivered a humiliating yet mercifully post-mortem wound. The evidence has been laid bare.

Not for me a noble burial. No royal robes, no gold or silver coin to prove my worth. No ceremony to ease my passing. Yet I am grateful I was not left to rot in some entirely unmarked spot. At least they carried me out of Bosworth Field.

As for my deformity, scorned by those at court – they think I did not hear them mock me – and unsightly though it was to others, it has proved a most useful and unique marker. My S-shaped curve made them catch their breath when they uncovered me. I made the hair on the nape of their necks stand up in recognition.

My bones speak for me. Each wound tells how I met my end, every piece of the struggle. My marrow speaks for me and tells you how I lived: meat and fish and fruit each day, no peasant's fare. My blood speaks for me. It has proved my identity.

Oh wondrous sight, they have rebuilt me! A more true likeness has never been known. Even the royal portraitist who stood before me did not capture it such as this. I am the picture of health, a youth in my prime: fresh complexion, raven's mane, eyes sparkling – a King in the making. It is as if I have sat up from the grave, dusted off centuries of grime, pulled on a fresh skin suit and stood before you once again.

The air spits and sparks, charged with expectation, as they prepare to tell those who have descended on this place: we have found him, we have found the lost King! I have bided my time and waited an eternity for this moment. See how well I have preserved the evidence? My history will be rewritten, my records revised, my story retold.

Now you know how I lived, how I died, where I was laid to rest. You have even looked me in the eye. But you will never know how I felt. You will never know of my dreams. The grey matter and beating heart have long since ceased to function and decayed to ash. Just know this: I am both a man of reason and of faith.

I have seen three seasons such as this but alas, all things must end, once more. I shall take my leave of you next spring when I am to be reinterred in a resting place more fitting for a King. Back to the cold, damp dark. My whereabouts will never be unknown again. My truth will echo down for five hundred years more. The very black and white of it, and all the grey areas in between, revealed. For it cannot be denied, my battle-scarred, crooked bones do not lie.

THE SAD TALE OF MARY SAWYER'S LITTLE LAMB

BY PHYLLIDA CLARKE

Heavy snow clouds darkened the horizon that morning. It was unseasonably late for such inclement weather in New England as Easter was only weeks away. Mary followed her father out into the fields to check the ewes and bring in the cows for milking. Their heavy leather boots crunched into yesterday's dusting of fine powdery snow which had frozen overnight.

Mary pulled her woollen shawl around her face to ward off the gnashing teeth of an Atlantic wind nipping her bright red cheeks. She nearly tripped over the body of a newly born lamb, still streaked with birthing blood and nearly pasted to the ground. Amazed that a mother could be so callous as to abandon her baby and go off to huddle with the rest of the flock, Mary bent down to feel the poor foundling for any signs of life. The parable of the one lost sheep came to her mind, and how the shepherd had forsaken all others to go search for it. The minister who came to school to teach them about the Bible had said that every soul is precious. His chilling eyes of grey steel would rake the room for any signs of a Doubting Thomas lurking behind the high wooden desks.

'Come on, Mary, keep up, it's too cold to be lingering,' her father called across the field. But Mary could just feel the feeble heart beating in that little chest. She threw off her shawl and wrapped it quickly around the lamb, grasping it to her, pulling her coat around it as best she could. 'Leave it, Mary, its mother has gone off with the others now, it hasn't a hope.' By this time the cows were gathering and heading for the barn, their breath going in white clouds before them, long horns shining with frost.

'Oh please, Father, I'm sure I can bring it back to life.'

'Leave it child, we have enough waifs and strays as it is.' He was flapping his arms up and down like Perky the Penguin trying to get the feeling to come back into his fingers, while keeping the cows moving forwards at the same time.

Mary had her mother's nature. The same stubborn streak that brought the Pilgrim Fathers over on the Mayflower almost exactly two hundred years before; they who carved farm land out of the wilderness with primitive tools and their Protestant determination. She hung back a little trying to breathe warm air into the lamb's face and lungs. Its body was limp in her arms. She rubbed it and shook it about inside her coat, praying that by the time she caught up with him her father would not notice that she had disobeyed him.

When she reached the barn, the cows were tied to their stanchions. Mary's father and two older brothers were crouched beneath them and beginning the rhythmical squeeze and pull, dragging the milk frothing into wooden pails between their knees. She hurried past the barn door, not stopping as she usually did to stir the mash or smell the new milk and listen to the contented sound of cows munching hay. Instead she went directly into the kitchen where her mother and younger brother Nat were pounding bread dough on the bare wooden planks of the kitchen table. Mary's mother wiped her hands on her apron, reached out for the lamb and tried joggling it about like she had many times with cold babies in the dead of night.

'Oh Mary, your soft heart will be the ruination of the family!' She looked at the little head lolling over her left arm. 'You could try some cat-nip tea but I don't give this one a great deal of hope.'

Mary spent a few hours trying to coax a suck from the cold muzzle of the wee lamb, cat-nip tea dribbling over her wrist and down into her sleeve. She stroked the motionless throat hoping to make it swallow something. She rubbed it with her own shawl, feeling the skin moving loosely over the tiny ribcage. She was sure it was the addition of a few spoons of sugar, sneaked into the brew when her mother wasn't looking, that eventually made it raise its own head and try a few sips of the warm liquid. Soon it was taking great gulps with gusto. In a while the lamb stood up, wobbled around, collapsed into a heap and tried again until it was able to support its own weight and totter around bleating and bumping into things.

Sometime later that day Mary had the wee orphan sucking new milk from a homespun teat, fashioned with the little finger of an old leather glove stitched into the corner cut from a flour sack. Mary's mother watched her feeding the lamb and thought of the hours she had spent rubbing beeswax into the tightly woven calico and over her tiny stitches so that the makeshift udder would hold milk for the many lost causes that came her way.

As time went on the lamb grew stronger and could be taken to a hurdled pen in the barn where Mary would go out and feed it before and after school. Eventually the spring melted into summer and the meadows were bright green once more. The lamb was put to live with the rest of the flock. It still bounced over to Mary bleating merrily whenever she appeared. She called it Ruth, Naomi's faithful daughter. Mary had the lamb so spoiled that it would never go back contentedly with the others but preferred to follow her around like a puppy. She groomed it daily removing the burdocks from its forelock and replacing them with pretty ribbons. She even thought it great sport to dress Ruth up in pantaloons and wrap a cape around the lamb's shoulders.

It was the custom for the Minister, Reverend Lemuel Capen, to call to the little schoolhouse in Sterling every Monday morning to ensure the children were properly versed in all their prayers and to check that their schooling was going as he would altogether wish it to. He would stand beside Miss Kimball at the front of the schoolroom and preach about the evils of slavery and how the wicked farmers in the Deep South were going mad for money with the price of cotton and sugar soaring way beyond the reach of ordinary people. How the Negro slaves were snatched from their homes and families in far away Africa, bound in chains, thrown into stinking ships and dragged out onto the quays in South Carolina, half-blinded from the darkness, starved and dying of thirst. How they were flogged through the town and sold to the highest bidder in the market square, children ripped from their mother's breast, families all scattered to the four winds. He thumped the desk with his riding crop, perspiration bursting from his quivering cheeks.

'They slave in the cotton fields and make the greedy farmers fat!' He seemed to stare straight at Mary and Nat, making them squirm on their hard benches, the tears burning their eyes and the guilt searing into their souls. Mary felt the cotton of her underslip to be like the forbidden fruit stolen from the very Garden of Eden. She thought of the spoons of sugar wastefully added to milk for orphan lambs. In her mind it all turned pink, tainted with Negro blood.

At last, when break time came, the mortified children fell out into the sun and ran off to hide in the shade under a big cedar tree. They could hardly bring themselves to eat their bread and drink their barley water for fear that the preacher would see them and remind them that as they ate and drank, little black children were starving in the fields where they toiled endlessly to make the fat men rich. Mary plucked bunches of grass from the wayside and fed it to the preacher's horse where it was tied to the railings. It swished at flies with its tail and stomped its front foot, raising dust. Mary reached up and stroked the glossy black neck, sucking in the smell of sweat and hot leather.

One such Monday morning Nat had the bright idea that

what they needed was a diversion to take the Minister's mind off misery. The happiest story he could think of was that of Mary's lamb Ruth who had been raised like Lazarus from the dead. The children decided it would be fun to dress Ruth in ribbons and a gingham apron and take the lamb to school to cheer everyone up. They brought her in early, washed her milky white fleece and combed out the tangles of the night. She looked so sweet in her little red-checked bonnet and bib. They set off together with Ruth trotting along beside them, bleating as she always did. They hauled her over the schoolyard wall and pushed her under the bench on which they sat. Mary covered her with a blanket and thought little more about her, enraptured as she was by the Reverend Capen's horror stories, which somehow always linked the 'evils of slavery' to the Old Testament and even Noah himself. This day the preacher had brought his young nephew John Roulstone, who was preparing to go to college in Boston. He stood, seemingly unmoved by the tales of black backs striped with blood from being whipped and bridles on men, followed inevitably by the pillars of salt and tablets of stone. Before the break time Miss Kimball, in an unexpected moment of zest, stepped up beside the preacher and asked who could recite the Lord's Prayer. She looked directly at Mary.

'I can, Miss,' Mary piped up and walked to the front of the school room with great reverence. Suddenly there was an almighty clatter, clatter, clatter on the wooden floor as Ruth bounded along behind her and the whole class burst into peals of laughter. Even Miss Polly Kimball could no longer keep a straight face.

'What's this then? Have you brought your flock to hear your prayers?' Reverend Capen sliced the jollity with his razor tongue.

'You'd best take it out, Mary.' Miss Kimball bent down slightly so as not to appear too fierce. But Mary was wishing at that moment for the great flood to swoosh into the room and swallow them all.

Young John Roulstone came to her rescue and said quietly, 'Come, Mary, I'll give you a hand.' She wanted to say, 'Thank you but I'm very well able to do it on my own,' however, she let him accompany her out into the dusty yard and lock the lamb into the privy. 'She'll be fine there till lunch time, you can take her home then,' he said quietly, his fingers pressing his nostrils together at the stench. Ruth's plaintive cries followed them back into the class.

Mary's mortification continued for the rest of the morning as the other students kept looking across at her and giggling. Young Roulstone stood with a stony-faced expression beside his uncle, trying to give the impression that he was taking it all in. The Reverend, however, did not let up for the remainder of the morning, rising finally to the story of Moses and Isaac, but rather than finishing the tale, he left them with the terrifying spectacle of the dagger in Moses' hand, raised above his terrified young son.

'Think on that!' he pronounced as he bowed his head and jammed down his wide-brimmed hat. His black gown swept past them and away he went into the shafts of light, leaving the door wide open for his nephew to follow.

That night Mary had nightmares about a knife in her hand and being ordered by her father to sacrifice the lamb. She sweated it out till morning when she ran to the field to check that all was well. Ruth came bounding over as always and butted her head against Mary's leg. The last thing she expected to see was John Roulstone riding over the horizon towards the farm.

'Who could this be now, coming at this time of the morning? It must be bad news,' her father said. He was bringing home the cows for milking. Mary ran out in front of them to greet her friend and Ruth followed close behind.

One of the cows was so alarmed by this that it snorted

and made a dash at Mary. She managed to dodge out of the way but saw with horror the Longhorn pin Ruth to the ground, then, with a sideways swing of its head, toss the lamb into the air.

For some time Mary sat on the ground, Ruth bleeding to death in her lap. It looked at her most pitifully as if pleading for her to do something to help. She knew of nothing she could do.

'Leave it down, Mary, you'll ruin your clothes. It won't live after a wound like that.' Her father's words were no comfort. He didn't wait around to persuade her. He knew better than to try and influence Mary in matters such as these and besides, the cows were cross enough already. But young John Roulstone dismounted from his horse, tied it to a railing and walked across the paddock to sit beside her. After some time he took a piece of paper from his waistcoat pocket.

'I brought you this poem; I thought the schoolchildren might like to hear it after yesterday.'

Mary laid the body of her pet beside her, wiped away her tears on the sleeve of her smock. She took the piece of paper, unfolded it with her blood-stained fingers and read it out loud.

'Mary had a little lamb,
its fleece was white as snow;
And everywhere that Mary went,
the lamb was sure to go.
It followed her to school one day,
which was against the rule;
It made the children laugh and play,
to see a lamb at school.
And so the teacher turned it out,
but still it lingered near,
And waited patiently about,
till Mary did appear.'

'That was most kind of you, Master Roulstone. Thank

you.' Together they buried the body in the garden and made a cross out of some pieces of timber. When she had changed her clothes they travelled to the school together, Mary riding behind John on his black horse. He did not go into the classroom but hung around outside to hear if the children laughed when they heard his poem. Miss Kimball was so disgusted by the blood smears on the paper that she put it flat on her desk and read from where it lay.

'Now get on with your lessons, children, and no more about it please.'

After lunch Mary noticed that the paper was gone. She never saw it again, nor John Roulstone. Miss Kimball did, however, tell them that God had intervened just in time and Isaac was spared. Pity he didn't do the same for Ruth, thought Mary.

JACK SPRATT

BY EILEEN CONDON

I knew my marriage was over when the auctioneer handed me the keys. Up to that moment, I still pictured the possibility of me and Tara being together, like we were in the old days. Our laughter came easy back then. Over time, it lost its edge, as we bought into the endless cycle of ballet lessons for our daughter and rugby training for our son. Our conversations with friends revolved around desirable addresses and one-upmanship with holiday destinations. The bills came fast and furious. Our once free and easy sex took on the feeling of just another chore to be added to the list of endless chores pinned to the freezer with a fridge magnet from Barcelona.

'It's all yours, now. Hope you're happy here.' With those parting words, the auctioneer started his '06 Mercedes and sped off, the registration a marker of better years for him too.

Rossmore House had belonged to one family for a couple of generations, but after the last member died it lay idle for many years. In the current market, demand for big homes 'with character' was low, so I got myself a bargain.

As a temporary measure, I decided to sleep in the library downstairs on a sofa bed I garnered from the division of marital spoils a week ago.

'Possession is nine-tenths of the law,' I quipped, as Tara stuck a yellow post-it with my name written on it on the arm of the sofa. 'God knows I've slept on it often enough for it to be mine.' It surprised me how much I wanted to hurt her, to deliver the parting shot. She looked at me with her arms crossed, then bent her head, and tucked a stray piece of hair behind her ear. When she lifted her head to look at me again, I searched her eyes for tears.

'If that's the game we're playing,' she said, enunciating the consonants at the end of each word, 'then Cooking for One: Volumes I-IV are mine.'

Venomous point-scoring was the next best thing to tears, I supposed.

The skies were clear on my first night in Rossmore House. I lay awake on the skinny foam mattress, the springs underneath digging into each shoulder blade. The blue-white light of the full moon shone through the bay window. My eyes scanned the bookshelves that ran along one entire wall. I got up and skimmed my index finger along the spines of the books, quick-reading titles in the moonlight. There were the usual heavy-hitters: Dickens, Hardy, Plato, Donne and Milton, but one volume stood out by its lack of a title. I pulled it out and opened the cover. Written across the top of the first page in cursive dark ink were the words: 'The Diary of John Spratt III.' I was intrigued, and read the first entry:

I have no one to talk to about certain matters, so I am keeping this journal as a way to stay sane. Mother has grown impatient about my lack of a partner. Father's death has accelerated her desire for a grandchild, and continuation of the family name. She's me driven demented, constantly trying to fatten me up, telling me no woman will choose a weedy wisp of a man. My confidence is low. There's talk now of an arrangement. A girl from a neighbouring county. Her family are of similar standing to ours. I hear her name is Joan.

That was enough information for one night. Besides, the battle scars from my DIY divorce had left me cynical about such matters. Marriage by choice was hard enough, but an arranged marriage seemed as enticing as root canal.

The next morning I began the job of clearing out the place. I flung remnants of former grandeur into a hired skip: a musty velvet-covered chair, a stained and yellowed silk lampshade, a broken umbrella stand. I kept thinking of

John and the pressure he was under. He probably married someone demanding and ended up broke. I felt a strong sympathy for a man I had never met. I worked hard the rest of the day. There were a few missed calls from Tara. It was a relief to know I was no longer obligated to answer them. I retired early and read more of John's diary:

Had first meeting with Joan. It was insufferable, mostly because we were like two specimens in a zoo. Family members stayed and had tea with us, pretending to talk to each other, but sneaking nervous looks our way. Joan seemed self-conscious when she was the first to finish her cold meat salad. She glanced at me a couple of times and offered a shy smile. She was a large woman, but her vulnerability showed a warmth I found oddly attractive.

Reading the last sentence, I was astounded. How could this man possibly feel fondness for a woman who was being forced upon him? Couldn't he see he was being set-up? I wished I could turn back the clock and say, 'Run, John, run!' It took me a while to fall asleep, despite being exhausted.

I rang Tara in the morning, asking her what she wanted in my best bored voice.

'I wanted to … see if … you were … ok,' she said.

I didn't respond well to her concern.

'What kind of a social-worker crap question is that?'

There was silence on the other end, and then a disconnecting tone. I wanted to throw the phone into the skip along with the rest of the rubbish.

Bit by bit, I worked on the house. My love of old, sprawling country estates was being challenged as I continued to sleep in the library rather than move into the master bedroom. It felt strange to sleep in the room where, presumably, the unhappily shackled couple were forced to cohabit. I had been too angry to read John's diary for a while, but took it up again a few weeks later:

The wedding was a simple affair, low-key, with no expense spared. Joan and I hardly spoke beforehand.

Strange, but when we exchanged vows, rather than call me John, as my mother always did, Joan said, 'I take thee Jack, to be my lawful wedded husband.' I felt Joan did this from a generous place in her heart, as if she understood I needed to be set free from some tight maternal grip. It was a singular action, but one that struck me in my soul.

Conniving bitch, I thought, but I read on. It appeared some time had passed before the next entry:

Joan and I have found a comfortable rhythm together, and I find this most strange, considering we never knew each other. Indeed, you could not get two people more opposite in physical appearance and tastes. And yet, there is a gratitude we feel for the other, and an overlooking of differences, that allows us to experience joy and peace together. As well as that, we eagerly await the day when we will have a child together, (our own little Spratt), and are busy making sure this happens quickly!

Well, I'll be damned, I thought. Jack and Joan were having a right ol' time upstairs and here was I lamenting Jack's fate. I worked hard outside, weeding and preparing the ground. Tara was on my mind all that day. I felt I owed her an apology from our last conversation. I rang her number and it went straight to voicemail.

'Hi Tara. It's me. Just wondering how you are? Sorry about the last phone call. I was clearing the garden here, and came across a rosemary bush. It reminded me of you and how much you liked to cook, even when sometimes it was just for one. Anyway, talk soon.'

I berated myself for sounding too smarmy, but it was done now.

I needed to finish reading that blasted diary because my head was swimming. Cop on to yourself, I thought. I went to the library and sat down in my new brown leather wing chair, befitting a bachelor. I took the diary from the shelf:

Joan was seen by the doctor today. We were told the dreadful news that she can never have a child. Mother is livid. I made sure Joan went to bed early, as she was so upset. I went downstairs, to find mother pacing back and forth in the parlour. I asked her what was wrong.

'We got a pig in a poke,' she said.

I grabbed her by the shoulders and pinned her against the wall. I was within a hair's breadth of striking her. I was so angry I could not speak. She continued:

'Listen to me now, Mr Jack Spratt. You will never get Rossmore House. You and your fat wife will be left destitute. You will rue the day you laid a hand on me!'

I write this knowing now that Rossmore will never have an heir and will eventually be sold. What once was important to me no longer holds any meaning. Bricks and mortar are no substitute for the love of a good woman. I have my Joan. Between us, our platter is full. I can only hope that the next occupant will be as lucky a man as I.

I sat in my wing chair all night long. I thought about my years with Tara. They had not been perfect, and I mistakenly expected perfection. When I wasn't getting it, I threw it all away. I had a lot to thank Jack for, and slumped in my chair, a humbled man.

First thing next morning, I drove to my old house and rang the doorbell. I couldn't wait to sort things out with Tara. She opened the door, wearing only a man's shirt that wasn't mine. I fumbled through the next few minutes, explaining how wrong I'd been, maybe how wrong we'd both been, resenting each other when things didn't go our way. I tried to tell her about Jack Spratt and his wife, and how they managed to overcome their differences, and live a long life together.

She listened with the same boredom I signalled to her in our phone conversation. Finally, when I was finished, she said,

'None of what you're saying is real. Don't you see? That stuff only happens in nursery rhymes.'

And then she shut the door.

THERE WAS AN OLD WOMAN

WHO LIVED IN A SHOE

BY NORA FARRELL

Everything changed the morning the old woman looked out her window and saw an absence of yellow. Her heart sank and she wasn't surprised when the twins, Petra and Pam, knocked on her door. Petra was carrying three sleeping pallets and young Tom was behind her holding his sisters Sally and Daisy by the hand.

'Morning, Grandma.' Tom winked.

The old woman winked back.

Pam had a folded playpen under one arm and a sleeping pallet under the other. Her baby, Janice, was peeping over her son Jack's shoulder.

'Can you mind our children?' the twins asked. 'We'll be back in yellow time.'

'Set the playpen up in the garden,' the old woman said. 'There will be no rain today.'

Pam unfolded it beneath a begonia bush and Jack placed his sister Janice inside and sat among the grasses to watch her.

The old woman opened her door wider. Petra, Pam, Tom, Sally and Daisy entered her tiny hall. Bedding was piled up in the corner of the spare room, changes of clothes stacked neatly in drawers. The twins leaned over and kissed their mother on the cheek.

'See you soon,' they said.

'It's never been as green as this. Use the hapnip carefully,' the old woman advised. She waved as her daughters disappeared over the brow of the hill. Then she locked the kitchen cupboard, dropped the key into her pocket and took a chair outside.

'You can't catch me,' Tom shouted and dashed away pursued by his sisters.

The old woman sat and watched her grandchildren chase each other around the begonia bush. Baby Janice clapped her hands in the playpen.

Green time continued and many of the old woman's neighbours followed her daughters to town. As long as the processing plant remained closed employment was scarce. As a result more and more children were left with her and she was forced to pay the snatchers for a new home. The shoe they brought her had belonged to a male human. It was brown and still shiny. The children gazed in awe as the home-conversion team set to work. Men climbed a ladder and tied the lace. Wooden room dividers were erected. Windows and a door carefully placed.

'I'll help,' Tom said, and painted the door hapnip yellow.

Furniture was moved in. Chairs were taken from the neighbours' houses and placed in the large kitchen. The old woman asked Sally to carry some of the precious hapnip which was transferred from one locked cupboard to another. It was on the highest shelf and food filled all the others.

In those days, once she finished her chores, Grandma taught the children how to play hopscotch and skipping. On the hottest days she took them swimming. Janice became a water baby. At night there was a sing-song interspersed with laughter. They all drank a diluted hapnip drink before bed.

'Time is becoming yellow,' Sally sang when the yellow dandelions bobbed their heads among the grasses. 'Soon Mama will be home.'

'Today is for wine-making,' Grandma said.

Tom threw a handful of dandelion petals at Jack.

'No waste,' Grandma said crossly. 'There'll be no wine for children who don't help.'

'Today is for butter-making,' she said when the yellow buttercups grew.

Her granddaughters, Sally, Daisy and little Janice, gathered around her. Six of the neighbours' children joined in when they saw buttercups stirred in water. The old woman tipped ingredients from her magic box into the mixture and tasty, slippery butter appeared.

On a day when it rained petals, yellow, pink, red and white floating around them, the old woman told the children to collect them for new clothes. Sally was the first to arrive home with her bag full. She poured the petals out carefully onto the windowsill and Grandma laid them out to dry.

'Can I have a red skirt?' Sally asked, imagining herself twirling in her gladioli outfit.

Grandma nodded. 'We called your mama Petra the petal gatherer. She was the best at that job and now you are.'

'Was she six too when she started?'

The old woman patted Sally's curls but didn't answer the question.

'Tomorrow I'm mixing hapnip with camomile for a special drink,' she said.

Sally saw the worry in Grandma's eyes. She slipped out and ran between the deserted boot and shoe homes to her parents' garden. She had dreamt of yellow but that day she didn't find what she was looking for.

Petra and Pam came to visit and glanced at each other with concern. The grasses were bleached by the sun but there wasn't a single hapnip to be seen.

'Mother looks tired,' Petra whispered.

'I'd love a cup of hapnip tea,' Pam said as she hugged Jack. Her son squirmed away from her.

'Not in front of the others,' he said and then added, 'There's been no hapnip for two weeks.'

Time changed from green to a mix of yellow and green, again and again. Baby Janice was now able to run but she had never known yellow time.

The old woman knew she was less agile and energetic than her own mother had ever been. Nevertheless, she continued to take a long walk every day. The clouds had been white and fluffy when she set out this morning but now they were grey and rain filled. She stopped and gazed uphill towards her shoe. Two days ago it had begun pulling apart at the heel, exactly where her bedroom was located. Only a portion of the tongue remained and the shoelace had shrivelled. She had been unable, so far, to acquire a replacement. Downhill the hapnip processing plant still stood idle, its paint peeling.

She pulled the wine flask from her pocket and shook it. 'Blast that,' she muttered to herself. 'There's not a drop left.'

She had only made one purchase in the hardware store, yet her bag grew heavy as she trudged home, the noise of the children giving her a headache and the first raindrops wetting her hair.

'It's almost time for the ant hunt,' she heard one boy say to another when she reached her garden.

'Never mind ant hunts,' she said to the eldest. 'Can't you see it's raining? Get inside and put out the buckets.'

When the boy didn't answer she surprised herself by her ability to grab him. She pulled his ear as hard as she could.

'Now!' she told him. 'You too, Master,' she said to his companion.

The boys disappeared through the open door.

She went into her bedroom, took the container of glue from her bag and hid it under the bed. Rain began bouncing off the window, dripping and rolling and drawing pictures on the pane. She placed an old towel at the heel, opened the window and yelled, 'Get in here now.'

The children were jumping up and down, sticking out their tongues and licking the raindrops. They dashed inside, tumbling over each other. One or two ran away into the pansies.

Water was dripping into buckets in the kitchen. The two boys who placed them there had disappeared. The old woman lined up five children as strictly as she could. She was relieved when Tom came in.

'Help Tom,' she ordered. 'And remember to place an empty bucket under the drips before you leave to pour out the full one.'

'We know that,' the nearest girl answered.

'You forgot last week, Miss,' the old woman said.

Miss and Master were the two words she used most often. She hoped it disguised the fact that she could no longer name all those who lived with her.

In the pantry most of the shelves were bare. There had been two full loaves in the bread bin this morning but only half a loaf remained. It was necessary to buy a new lock and ensure food was doled out in her presence. She had so many children she didn't know what to do. It was easy to tell who grabbed food but what could she do? Some of them were too fat and others too thin. On bath day she knew little Hazel was washed more than once and that others escaped altogether. They shouted and played and fought each other for hours on end. The bedroom was the only place she could find any peace so she stayed in there for an hour a day with the door locked. The mirrors had been removed when the hapnip face cream ran out. One glimpse of herself had been more than enough.

The rain stopped, mercifully, and bucket duty ended. She sat her grandchildren and six of the others at the kitchen table. The rest sat on cushions on the floor. She gave them some broth and one thin slice of bread each. They complained that it was not enough. Two of the girls had their pigtails tied together by one of the boys. A girl drew a picture with chalk on the table.

'I told you lot to behave,' the old woman shouted and took out her bamboo. They jumped up and ran outside. She was too tired to follow.

'Her legs hurt and make her cranky,' Tom explained as he put his arms around his sisters. Daisy sucked her thumb. When the old woman returned to her room, Sally tiptoed behind her. She took the towel from the floor and wrung it out the window, then turned to her grandma.

'Did you get the glue?'

Grandma nodded. Two rainy seasons had passed since she started saving.

The next morning, sunlight blazed into the bedroom. She opened the window and heard a butterfly pass by. A patch of dandelions had sprung up overnight and children were already racing among them. The old woman drank her tea and stepped outside. She carefully opened the can of glue, dipped a brush into it and began painting her home. She put extra on the heel to ensure her bedroom was waterproof again. Sally helped until her hand was too tired to continue. Then Tom came and took the brush.

'Off you go, Sal.' He smiled. 'I'll take over now.'

The shelves in the pantry were completely empty. Not a single crumb remained in the bread bin. The old woman put a pot of broth on the stove and began stirring it.

'I'll stir,' Tom said. 'There are plenty of dandelions for wine.'

'It's too late now to make it.'

'But I'll chop them down.'

'Not today. Set the table. I'll keep stirring.'

'But Grandma...'

'No buts out of you or you can go live elsewhere. You're old enough.'

Tom opened the press and took out five wooden bowls at a time. 'I can't see the point of spoons. Half our lot don't use them.'

'Put them out anyway. At least I'll have shown you the right way to do things. Dinner!' she shouted through the open window.

The children rushed in, tumbling and laughing. She gave them some broth without any bread. They complained that it was not enough. One boy dipped his spoon into his bowl and flicked broth at the girl beside him. She poured the contents of her bowl over his head and then cried because there was nothing else to eat.

'We want more!' one group shouted, pointlessly banging their spoons on the table.

'I told you lot to behave,' the old woman yelled, took out her bamboo, whipped them all soundly and sent them to bed.

Sally was singing and hopping from foot to foot under the begonia bush.

'What are you so happy about?' Tom asked her.

'I have something to show you. Follow me.'

Sally ran and Tom ran after her. She brought him behind the deserted shoe where they were born. The shoe was shrivelled to nothing but the crop was wonderful.

'It was safer here than in Grandma's garden.'

'You've been caring for these alone? Sally, you're a marvel.' The garden had been silent apart from the flutter of butterfly wings. Now peals of laughter echoed in the air.

'I'll tell Grandma now,' Sally said, running back the way she had come.

'Grandma,' Sally said.

The old woman stretched and sat up in the bed. The child's eyes were twinkling under her pink snapdragon hat. Her right hand clutched basil, oregano and tender chive shoots.

'You found something to flavour the broth. You're a great girl. Tasty broth and dandelion wine. Today will be a good day.'

Sally laughed, placed the herbs on Grandma's eiderdown and opened the bag she had in her left hand. The sweet smell wafted around the room. Grandma put her nose to the bag, inhaled deeply and giggled. Hapnip, she couldn't believe it! She hugged Sally again and again.

She squeezed juice from the hapnip stem and rubbed it on her arms, legs and lower back. The rest she poured into a jar.

Outside children played hopscotch and chase the bee. Their play made her smile for the first time in many moons. She clasped Sally's hand and walked with her to the row of deserted shoes. The yellow glow made her heart sing. The crop was plentiful enough to re-open the processing plant.

'Run to the bakers, Tom,' the old woman said, taking a coin from her apron pocket, 'and buy all the bread you can carry.' Then she kissed Sally, knelt and touched the delicate yellow flower of the hapnip.

That night Grandma danced a little.

'I used to be able to turn and twist,' she said. 'And I could leap over stools.'

'Like this!' Sally said, taking a jump.

'Exactly like that and soon I will do it again.'

A note was tied to a hoverfly and sent to Petra and Pam. 'Yellow time has begun, come home and have fun.'

When the hoverfly had departed she turned to the children with a chuckle.

'Be seated Misses and Masters,' she said, then gave them some broth with plenty of bread, hugged them all soundly and sent them to bed.

ROCK A BYE BABY

BY MAJELLA GORMAN

I stand at the kitchen window and glimpse the November sun filtering through the trees. I see Jack rake fallen leaves. Retirement suits him. His hands, once white and pristine, now grip the rake with a ruggedness of comfort and ease. I watch him fill the wheelbarrow, move it towards the compost heap and tip it. He has poured love into this garden and his love has been reflected back. Jack's passion and enthusiasm swept me along over three decades ago when we decided to buy the old rectory with the yew tree at the bottom of the garden. 'A fresh start,' Jack had said. Over time we began to call it home as we raised our daughter Beth.

I shudder, button my cardigan, but know I cannot insulate myself against the coldness that I feel this morning. I let my hands fall into the sudsy water and rinse the breakfast vessels. I am filled with a desire to bring warmth to the kitchen. I stoke the fire, open the presses and gather my ingredients. My hands find their rhythm as I mix and add. I place the cake in the oven. Soon the air is filled with the mingling of nutmeg and cinnamon. It's time to collect the eggs. I walk down to the hen house. The hens have not disappointed me as I fill my bowl. I take a moment to watch them as they peck their way around the gravel.

Jack's mobile phone rings and I hear him greet Mike. I walk towards him, happy that we have become closer to our son-in-law over the last twelve months. I watch Jack raise his free hand and run it over the top of his head.

'We'll have the room ready, course ye can come down,' I hear Jack say.

'What is it, what's wrong?' I call out.

Jack places the phone back in his pocket and stands in front of me.

'It's Beth … she's … she's had a miss…'

I let the bowl of eggs fall and watch them crack as they hit the stone path.

'We didn't even know…' I begin.

'Just eight weeks.'

'No … no…' I say.

He bends to pick up the empty bowl and guides me back into the house. Silence sits between us. He busies himself with the kettle and places a mug of tea in front of me.

'We have to be strong for them,' he says.

'I can be, haven't I been strong all my life? I felt it this morning from the moment I put my feet on the floor.'

'And you were right.'

'I'd prefer if I wasn't.' I rise to prepare the room for Beth and Mike.

From the upstairs room I hear Jack going out in the car. Extra supplies have to be got. I dust the dresser and straighten the ornaments and childhood trinkets. I feel Beth's pain. I tidy the rocking horse into the corner of the room and I see Beth as a child, chubby legs climbing onto it. At the end of the bed I see her lining up her teddy bears for a tea party. I begin to dust the window ledge and see Beth following her father around the garden; chasing a butterfly to find out where it lives. Beth, an only child, constantly encouraged to invite her friends home to play. Summer days spent running around the box hedging, transforming it into their magical fairy kingdom. The swing, visible through the bare branches, looks forlorn. Will we ever hear the sound of children playing in this garden again?

I move from Beth's room into my own bedroom, open the press and take down the tissue-wrapped parcel. I sit on the bed, unwrap it and remove the yellow crocheted baby blanket. I place the blanket against my cheek and nuzzle it. This blanket does not hold the scent of a new-born baby. I remember that morning when my body failed me, the searing pain, the knowingness, the emptiness. I gather the blanket close to me, the need for air overcoming me. I walk the familiar path to the yew tree and sit on the seat that Jack placed there many years ago. I beg the yew tree to let its wisdom and strength flow into me again. I sit for a while and then hear Jack's car returning. He joins me on the seat.

'I haven't seen that blanket in a long time,' he says.

'You know about this?' I begin to say.

'I know that you never crocheted again.'

'I was full of hope, nights as I sat crocheting. I had just finished it the day before. Always thought it was my fault; too early to be making baby clothes.'

'Annie, it was never your fault,' Jack says.

'I used to sit here and wonder about that baby.'

'And I used to watch you, lost in your own world, unable to reach you.'

'I longed to know if it was a boy or a girl.' My hands smooth out the delicate fabric.

'And I longed to help you, Annie. As the weeks passed by and the seasons changed I began to see that you were getting stronger and stronger. It was then that I placed another garden seat opposite this tree.'

'Jack, I sat over there when I didn't feel the need for the protection of the yew tree.'

'And that is how we got through those days.'

'But we never spoke about it … properly, I mean.' I reach out and place my hand over his.

'We didn't have to. Our actions spoke. Beth and Mike will be ok too,' Jack says.

I see a tear slip down his face and I too let my tears fall, unshed tears for our baby of thirty-three years ago.

'I got some tulip bulbs, let's plant them, they'll be lovely in the spring,' Jack says.

'My favourite flowers.'
I fold the blanket to return it to its home in the press.

A Patch of Faded Blue

by Patrick Griffin

How I dread the hollow summer which stretches ahead. There is something dead about a school at term's end. The last of my students have bolted home. I take one final look. Only the sound of my shoes slapping on the marble floor breaks the silence. I leave the corridor and lock the door.

My briefcase is full of last term's books and today's half-eaten sandwich. I walk the long route home.

I know that when I finally open my front door, you, my devoted wife, will ask as you always do at the end of term each year, 'And how was school today? Excited about your holidays?'

You will say it to me as if I am six years old and coming home after my first term at school.

'And did you go out with all your nice teacher friends to celebrate the first day of your school holidays?' you will ask.

Last year I lied to you. It was easier that way. I did not tell you that I went alone to Madigan's Bar. Instead I told you that I had gone with my colleagues to the Royal Hotel and, at your urging and insistence, I filled in all the details of my imaginary lunch.

'And did you sit next to the School Principal and discuss all your ideas for next term?' you asked.

I had told you anything that would keep you happy.

'And were you a naughty boy and did you have a little tipple?' you asked.

I assured you that I only ever touched a drop on very special occasions, and even then only a small drop.

You leaned towards me. Through your uneven, tobacco-stained teeth, you whispered, 'Aren't you better off without it?'

And then you pinched my cheek.

I had hoped that you wouldn't get so close to me that you'd smell the mask of mint sweets and mouthwash on my breath. I was careful with my diction. I did not want to slur my words. But I knew I could handle a few mouthfuls of strong liquid comfort before it became too obvious.

'Take Uncle Willie, for example…' you said.

And then you dragged out your family's dirty linen for another year's airing. You relayed the story of how your Uncle Willie drank the family out of house and home. How, in time, he saw the error of his ways and became a changed man. You made references to the Prodigal Son and how we all can change and become better people. And I wondered if you expected me to be something other than what I was. I pretended to listen intently to your droning. Over the length of your ever-embellished family saga, I drifted in and out of your tale. I nodded sagely every now and then at various points in your monologue. Occasionally I muttered something or other I hoped would be appropriate. You felt better for having got across your lesson on moderation.

'I've made your favourite meal,' you said, 'with a special treat for you today.' And you leaned ever closer to me and whispered, 'Ice-cream and jelly!'

I wanted to scream at you, 'I am not six years old. I am closer to sixty. Get that into your silly head, woman!'

But I did not scream. I did as you expected. So we sat and ate. I was careful not to spill anything on your embroidered tablecloth, spread out for special days, you told me. I ploughed my way through a dish which vaguely resembled bacon and cabbage and your excitement built up as we approached dessert. You watched with unconcealed delight as I dipped my spoon into my glass bowl with its chipped edge. You flinched as a blob of jelly trickled down my chin and dropped onto the tablecloth.

'Silly boy,' you muttered as you dabbed my chin with

your napkin. That silent scream built up in me again and I wondered if I could face the long days ahead.

You told me that the fire was lit and my slippers warmed. I wanted to yell at you that I was almost sixty years old, not ninety-six, and that I liked my slippers cold. But I nodded in feigned appreciation and sat at the fire which seemed to have lost its will to live.

'Oh, you are a naughty boy!' you scolded me. 'You have not finished the snacks which I put in your lunchbox this morning.'

I froze when I saw you putting away my briefcase and lunchbox. Had you found the empty whiskey bottle? I thought fast. In a flash I played back the events of the previous few hours. The supermarket. Yes, I remembered the supermarket, where I had put a packet of raisins, some sultanas and a small bottle of cheap whiskey into the basket. I remembered what I had said to the young lady at the checkout.

'It's for my wife. For her cakes. The whiskey, I mean.'

I felt a rush of blood to my face and wondered why I couldn't keep my mouth closed. The girl at the checkout looked up and smiled. Now I felt I had made it all too obvious.

'She treats you well. You're a lucky man.'

I wondered what she meant. She saw my puzzlement and she continued, 'Your wife. She must be making a lot of cakes lately.'

I was certain that everyone in the queue must have heard. She put my purchases into a paper bag. At the first opportunity I dumped the raisins, sultanas and the crumpled bag into a rubbish bin and transferred the whiskey to my briefcase.

I gathered my thoughts and realised that you were still talking and complaining about how I managed to fill the corners of my briefcase with crumbs and crusts and stale biscuits. You did not mention the empty whiskey bottle. Then I remembered. The bottle bank! Yes! That was where I dropped the bottle. Where I drop all the whiskey bottles.

Now I am almost half way home.

I realise that summer will drift on, punctuated by the unnecessary jobs you will find for me. Last year you asked me to paint our faded blue front door. Somehow I never got round to it. Each morning, just like last year, I will check if the postman has delivered anything for me.

'Are you sure there's nothing wrong? Is there something you're not telling me? You're so jumpy these days,' you will say to me.

And I will assure you that I am only waiting for the postman to arrive.

'Are you expecting something special?'

I will lie to you and say that I'm not waiting for anything in particular, only the usual stuff from the Department about pensions and entitlements. I will check each day's delivery of bills and junk mail and unrequested catalogues and dread the arrival of one particular letter.

One morning you will say to me, 'Is this what you are looking for?' and you'll hand me a letter.

'Open it!' you will urge and I will tear the side of the envelope and peer inside. The words 'Teachers' Night Out' will shout at me from the corner of a gilt-edged card and I will want to die.

If I go you will make me wear my sensible out-of-date tweed jacket with the leather patches which hide the frayed elbows. I will feel old and shabby and will try to stay on the edge of the gathering throng and fade away.

Last year I went, just to keep you happy.

I had hoped that I could slip away quietly at a suitable moment. Nobody would have noticed my absence. But just as I tried to leave I was approached by a bright young thing who looked young enough to be one of my pupils. There was something familiar about her face. I tried to rack my brain to figure out who she was and her name continued to elude me.

Soon she was joined by her friends and I tried to find the appropriate place in their conversation when I could make my escape. That bright young thing rescued me from my misery and reminded me that she taught English literature in the classroom next to mine, and that she passed me in the corridor at school each day. She told me how she and her partner were considering buying a holiday home in Portugal or the South of France or somewhere exotic where they could hop across for the occasional weekend. She raised a quizzical eyebrow and asked me what properties I might be viewing. I told her that I was really thinking about putting in double-glazed windows. But that wasn't quite the same thing. Was it?

She told me about her summer in Biarritz and her skiing exploits. Her friends compared their trip to Paris that year with the previous year's safari in Kenya. They looked at me, the man in the tweed jacket, and waited for me to tell them of my summer exploits.

I told them that I went with you to a beach on the west coast. One of them asked me was it Malibu or Santa Monica and I told her that it was on the other west coast.

I did not say that it rained for the whole week on Achill Island and that you and I sat inside our rented caravan and sipped countless cups of tea while we waited for the sun to come out. Nor did I tell them that when you asked me each day to get you the morning paper, I also managed to find time to have a quick drink before I got back with your daily news and a bar of your favourite dark chocolate. I did not mention that I had chewed mint sweets to make my breath fresh and to hide my sin.

You will still be asking me about that letter.

'Is it?' you'll continue. 'Is that the letter you're expecting?'

Again I will lie and tell you that I am not expecting anything at all and that this is just another piece of junk mail. I will fold back the corner of the envelope covering the words 'Teachers' Night Out' and I will tear the envelope and card to shreds. I'll toss the pieces into the fire and for a moment the gilt lettering will flare up and mock me. Then, it will curl up and spark itself into nothingness.

Now I am almost home. When you see me you will lean towards me and through your uneven, tobacco-stained teeth, you'll whisper, 'Something special for you today. Ice-cream and jelly!' And then you'll pinch my cheek.

I have reached my house.

I turn the key in my faded blue door.

I want to scream.

NEEDLES AND PINS

BY MARY HEALY

Growing up I watched swathes of fabric being transformed into clothes. The promise of patterns intrigued me; pieces of fine tissue pinned and tacked with long, spidery stitches. I remember the tension of that moment, scissors poised, before Mother made the first cut, for when fabric was cut there was no going back. Sometimes, after school, I sat in the room where she worked and watched her fit the clothes. Ladies peeled off their blouses and skirts and stood in their slips, arms rigid in the air. Mother carefully lowered the clothes over their heads, hoping the tacking threads would hold, that the pattern would align correctly, hoping most of all that the customer would like it. The customer, meanwhile, held her breath and I held mine, not sure why or for what.

Few knew of the scraggy ends of tangled threads or the place where seams met and were steamed into neat obedience. These were invisible, concealed under the drape of shiny lining, quietly holding the garment in place and hiding soft pliable flesh.

I remember the secrets they told her, why the summer dress could not be fitted anymore, maybe when the child arrives. Some told of drinking husbands and sisters in poor circumstances. Others whispered of women's problems. Tales of wombs, wayward sons and lost babies drifted around the room. The secrets they could not share behind the confessional grille were the ones my mother absolved. As they undressed I noticed how they changed. Something fell away from them with the importance of their clothes. It rested on a waiting chair and, as they stood there, even the hardiest and wealthiest characters had a naked vulnerability about them.

That summer, mother made a wedding dress for Miss Walsh; she worked in the library and came for fittings on Thursdays. The parlour was specially cleaned and then the parcel arrived and was carefully laid onto the table. Coarse hairy twine held layers of thick brown paper, inside a layer of the finest tissue like frosted cobweb and finally the wedding gown fabric. The room filled with a lustrous reflected light and it made a shushing sound when it was moved on the table.

'She got it from Paris. She has an aunt in a convent over there. White satin. Look.' She pointed to a design. 'Embroidered, all hand done by French nuns. It will make up beautifully.'

Miss Walsh was slim with long blond hair. She was like a newly made garment, neat, pressed, waiting to be collected. When she came for a fitting she undressed behind the screen and then walked out shyly. Between fittings the dress was carefully hung under a sheet in a corner. There was talk about flowers and the cake and wedding arrangements and I listened as the dream unfolded. The reception was to be in her home place and there was great work with the garden and the house was being repainted. Miss Walsh came to fit the dress at various stages, more often as the wedding date approached.

One day she arrived, driven by a fair-haired man. He sat in the car and read the paper while she had her fitting. I watched him from my bedroom window. This was the man all the arrangements were for. This was the man Miss Walsh would spend the rest of her life with. As he read the paper he smoked a thick cigar. The smoke rose up in the air and I could smell it, a rich, dark aroma. This smoke had been in his mouth, breathed through his lips and now it reached out and caressed my face, touched my skin and reached inside me so gently, so tentatively, so insistently. I wondered what it would be like to have a handsome man wait for me, open the car door and kiss me tenderly on the cheek, as he did when Miss Walsh came out from her fitting.

The last day Mother helped her into the dress she looked perplexed, there seemed to be something wrong, the slim waistline didn't seem to sit right. Miss Walsh looked embarrassed, even more than she usually did when she emerged from behind the screen. Then she began to cry.

'Helen, would you collect the eggs?' It was far too early to collect the eggs and I was about to tell my mother this when I caught her eye.

They were longer than usual with the fitting, so long that Mrs Dooley from the post office had arrived and was waiting in the kitchen. She was having a suit made, a serviceable donkey-brown worsted wool suit with inverted pleats.

'She won't be long now, Mrs Dooley. She's just with another customer.'

Mother had warned me never to discuss people's business.

'Who has she in there?'

'I couldn't tell you, I was doing the hens, but I'm sure she won't be long.'

'Maybe I'll pop my head in.'

'No need, Mrs Dooley. She will call you when she's ready. Anyway, the ironing board is in the way, you won't be able to get in for the moment.'

We heard the front door close and Mrs Dooley was on her feet, peering out the window, her chubby fingers parting the geraniums.

'Ah, the wedding,' she said. 'I remember that parcel coming from France, the weight of it. Her aunt, the nun, sent it over. They have a lot of nuns and priests in that family, they're very proud people.' She repeated this to my mother when she went into the room.

'They're very fine people, indeed.' Mother agreed.

Mrs Dooley struggled out of her blouse and shook her skirt to the floor. There was no need for Mrs Dooley to be shy for underneath she was like a stout, well-upholstered chair with layers of elasticised garments. Small cushions of flesh escaped out over the tops and sides of these clothes.

'The family is very keen on this match; apparently she was involved with someone else…' she flicked a glance in my direction '…unsuitable … and they were very worried. This chap's family is very well off. Her uncle, the bishop, is supposed to be marrying her. Of course, they're no better than any of the rest of us at the end of the day, for all their airs and graces.'

A few days later Mother called me into the parlour.

'Come here, pet, and let me try this on you. Miss Walsh had to cancel. You're about the same height.' She lifted the gown over my head and I felt the world shift to ice-white wonder. The fabric was cool and whispered as it passed my ears.

For a moment the dark parlour disappeared and I was in the world of Snow White and Cinderella. My head popped through the opening and I faced my mother in surprise. Eye to eye we met. She smiled. Behind her in the mirror I looked at a girl in a white wedding dress, a tall, slim girl with dark hair and big, brown eyes. I was Cinderella going to the ball.

'I'm going to wear a dress like this when I get married.' I pulled in the vacant fabric in the bosom area and peered down at my kneeling mother.

'Are you now?' she said.

'Will you make my wedding dress when I grow up?'

'Steady now,' Mother said from near the floor. She looked up at me. 'That'll be a while yet. Maybe we'll make it together.'

The phone in the hall rang.

'Don't stir.' Her finger wagged at me and her eyebrows raised.

I gathered the fabric in my hands and lifted the gown wide as my arms could stretch. The image in the mirror curtseyed and sashayed and her smile widened. The fabric gleamed and shone. It reflected the whiteness of her teeth, made her skin glow and her eyes shine. I could hear Mother's voice on the phone.

'Ah no, really, are you sure?' The conversation continued at length and I was tired standing there. I was really thirsty too and began to think about the drinks and goodies on the pantry shelf nearby. The more I thought about them the more I wanted something. If I walked very carefully I could get what I wanted. One more look at the door. Mother's voice was quiet now, something really interesting, she was going to be a while.

'Ah, that's terrible. When did she go?'

I tiptoed out to the pantry, carefully lifting the sides of the gown so it wouldn't touch the floor. The table was covered in food, a bowl of red jelly still steaming where it was left to cool. My eyes rose to the high shelf where lemonade, orange and Ribena bottles were stored. If I stood up on the small step I could just about reach it.

Behind me the door opened from the kitchen and Father's head appeared.

'Oh sorry...' he began, 'I didn't see...' Then he stopped when he realised it was me. His eyes swept over the gown then back to my face.

'Well, look at you,' he said. 'You're all grown up looking.'

I smiled back at him, stood there to be admired, stood there in that big, stiff, white dress.

'What are you doing?' he whispered.

My eyes slid up to the bottles.

'Your mother will kill you if she finds you out here in that.'

'I know, but I wanted a drink,' I said, 'and she's on the

phone for ages.'

'Right.' He was different with me, shy, strange, as if I was someone else. 'Here, I'll get some for you, some of this?'

I nodded, shy myself in the formal dress. He poured the Ribena into a glass, splashed some water in to dilute it.

'Now careful,' he said, 'for the love of God.'

I took the glass and sipped it, then we heard the phone click and our eyes met.

'Here,' I said, pushing the glass towards him.

He reached but never got there. The glass fell in a terrible, slow, wide arc in the air between us. Drops of dark red liquid flew towards me, onto the pristine white gown.

As we stood there I could hear my mother's footsteps approaching. The door opened and Mother took in the scene.

'Take it off,' she said quietly. 'I don't think she will need it now.'

Some weeks later I was on a school tour. Winding our way across the country we watched small villages and towns come to life. Shops were opening and bundles of newspapers lay slumped at their doors.

Passing through one of these towns the bus slowed momentarily. You could see into people's back gardens, their morning kitchens, untidy breakfast tables. It was then I saw Miss Walsh. She was leaving a house and a man in bare feet was standing at the door. He was dark-haired, greying at the temples. She walked away from him, stopped, then turned back swiftly and they kissed, standing there in the rain. It was not a gentle kiss; there was something awkward, desperate and clumsy about it. He had his fingers roughly twined through her hair and she looked tossed, crumpled, untidy. As the bus pulled away, I saw them turn back into the house and close the door. A gust of wind blew the last cherry blossoms from a tree in the garden. It fell like confetti, lost in the long, overgrown grass.

THREE BLIND MEN

BY ORLA HENNESSY

15th October 1555, Oxford, England

The stone walls around me weep and the damp air chills my bones as I walk along the passageway and down the steps of Bocardo prison.

For over three years I have worked here as a gaoler, but my life was very different before we moved into Oxford twelve years ago. At that time Henry VIII took over the monastery lands. My parents, brother and I had worked as tenant farmers on the monks' land, so when I was fifteen we were forced to leave and move into the town to get paid work. I have grown used to my new situation, but in the evenings after breathing foul air all day I long for the freshness of the countryside. In spring on the farm the air smelled of wild flowers and herbs, in summer new cut hay, and in autumn the barn filled with the aroma of barley and apples resting in their bulging sacks. By this time of year all our produce would be sold to the monks and supplies bought to last us the winter. Right now I would be chopping wood and stacking it by the barn wall. Instead I am choosing my footsteps through the mud and waste on the streets of Oxford town as I make my way home.

When I open the door to our rooms my mother Ellen is standing at the table cutting bread.

'Is all well, Mother?' I ask, as I remove my jerkin and knee boots.

'Yes, Yon. With you?' she answers, taking a bowl from the table and ladling pottage into it.

'Well enough, Mother.'

I wash my face in a pail of water, a country habit my

mother still insists on, go to the fire and rasp my hands together.

'Winter has come early,' I say.

'I dread it, Yon. I feel the cold more and more.'

I sit down as she fills a bowl for herself.

'I will get more wood to put by this year,' I say. 'Much will be used at the stake tomorrow.'

She sits opposite me. We bless ourselves, thank God for our food, and eat.

'It is a terrible way to die,' she says. 'But, they had their chances. They would not recant, and this is the result.'

I wipe my bowl with a crust of bread and chew on it.

'They believe what they believe, Mother. They don't deserve to die for that.'

'Not for their faith. No. But for what their like did to us and all our neighbours.'

I sigh. 'Let us not speak of this again, Mother.'

She finishes her supper in silence and takes the bowls away. I sit on a fire stool and hold my head in my hands, feeling the heat soak into my crown.

'I cannot help thinking of it all,' she continues. 'Of your father and brother and how everything has changed.' Her voice rises. 'My poor John and our Ralph might not have died if we were still on the farm.' She wraps the bread in a cloth and thumps the bundle onto the table.

I turn around to face her. 'Mother. That was a long time ago. And we cannot do anything about it.'

I hope she will leave it be.

Then she sighs. 'Maybe the monks will come back. Perhaps Queen Mary will persuade them. We can work the land again and all will be well.'

She is staring into space now, her eyes bright and a little smile on her face.

'It will not happen, Mother,' I say in a firm voice. 'Things can never be as they were. The monks have gone to France. Queen Mary and Prince Philip own all the farmland. She is now the farmer's wife.' The image of Queen Mary in her heavy embroidered gown carrying pails of slop to the pigs almost makes me laugh. Mother comes out of her reverie and sits on a stool beside me, her face long and grey.

'I'm sorry, Mother. But you know it is useless to think of it. If you could only take things as they are now, you would be more at peace.'

'I try. I try, but it unsettles me. Over and over.'

'All we can do is wait, and hope for better times. For now I will work in the prison to pay our rent. And I will bless myself as often as I must while Mary is Queen. But please do not talk about her. The more I see of these executions and how convinced the Protestants are, I think we are better off with them.'

A deep frown marks her forehead.

'How can you say that when they have taken our livelihoods from us?'

'Yes, they have. But you forget, the monks were not saints either. They made much coin from our goods, and often refused our wool when they knew we had no other market for it. Was that Christian?'

'But we never wanted reform,' she went on, ignoring my point, 'we want the old religion back, the old rituals. We never wanted to break with Rome.'

'And now Queen Mary has brought you back under Rome. So be content with that.'

Mother is silent at last. Then she blesses herself, passing her calloused hands slowly over her face.

'Try not to fret, Mother. Our faith itself is all that really matters.'

She stands up.

'But yours is not the one true faith any more. You have become blind like those Protestants.'

'Mother, I will not discuss this again. You believe what you will, and you must allow me to do the same.'

'I will pray for you, Son, and for Father Latimer and

Master Ridley. I will say my rosary.'

'Yes, Mother.'

'Goodnight, Yon.'

She takes the rush light, goes to the other room and closes the door. I lie down on my cot to rest. Our neighbours overhead have not retired yet and I hear their footsteps trace patterns across the floor. One heavy and hard, the other light and shuffling. From where I lie I can see the whole room and its contents casting shadows in the firelight. The table and benches, the dresser brought from the farmhouse, too big for this place, the pile of clothes for sewing by the window where my mother sits while working. Beside me, what I value most is the small pile of books including Tyndale's English Bible, from which I learned to read and write. I give thanks as I do every night for my uncle George, a man of means who favoured me with schooling for some years until I was obliged to work on the farm. I read a few passages from the Bible and fall asleep.

On my way to the prison the next day the streets are crowded. Many carry staffs and trudge tiredly, their shoes and clothes covered in mud. Outside the inn, riders from London stand in groups talking. They are dressed in embroidered breeches and doublets, fine woollen cloaks and feathered caps. Cripples and beggars approach the strangers and are chased away. Peasants, barefoot and bareheaded, walk towards the city gate to take up positions near the stake that they might have a good view.

I go out to see the site where the two bishops, Latimer and Ridley, are to be executed today. The earth around the area is scorched and strewn with blackened stones and charred stumps. The stake is surrounded by straw, gorse and bundles of faggots. Strong chains hang from it. There is a gap at the side for the prisoners to be brought in and tied up. I can sense the spirits of the many men and women who have been tortured and executed here over the past year and I pray for them.

When I arrive in the armoury it is packed with men-at-arms brought in especially for the day. Prison governor Woodson calls out the names of three gaolers to accompany him. Myself and two others.

'We will take Cranmer to the tower at the North Gate to witness the executions,' he says. 'He is to witness all of it, from start to finish. Understood?'

We answer yes.

'I will be back in a while. Wait here,' he instructs us.

The crowded room is loud with talk and the clanking of armour, and thick with the smell of sweat and leather.

Will leans in to me, speaking low. 'These men are all over three score years. Does Bloody Mary's cruelty know no bounds?'

'It would seem so,' I say.

We put on our gloves and helmets.

'This has nothing to do with Cranmer's religion,' Rob says. 'She is punishing him for what he and her father did years ago.'

'Do you mean when he helped Henry divorce her mother?' Will asks.

'Yes. That made Mary a bastard, and so she lost her place in line to be Queen. Now that she is, she will make him suffer for it.'

'Hush,' I say, alarmed that they would speak of this here. 'Her spies are everywhere.'

We take our bills and wait for the governor at the door. When he returns we follow him to the bishop's cell. I open the door. Cranmer is kneeling beside his cot, bare-headed, arms leaning on the edge, head bowed.

'You will come with us to the North Tower,' Woodson says to him.

Cranmer struggles slowly to his feet and stares at him.

'For what reason?' he asks.

'You will witness the executions,' the governor answers.

Cranmer's face grows pale. 'Witness?'

'Her Majesty commands it.'

Woodson waits. He has been kind to Cranmer and is clearly uncomfortable with this instruction.

'I see,' Cranmer says quietly. He puts on his black velvet cap and outer cloak, leaving his long white beard hanging outside his garments. He follows Woodson and we follow him. He is ordered to stand at the edge of the parapet overlooking the broad ditch where he has full view of the pyre and the large crowd that has gathered. I see among them many clergy and the Spanish friars who try to persuade Protestants to recant. I have learned that people attend executions for different reasons: to support the wretched, to see justice done as they see it, or because it entertains them.

Men-at-arms are posted around the area of the pyre to keep the people back. Within this ring the High Sheriff of Oxfordshire Lord Williams and the Mayor and commissioners sit on a row of chairs. Their colourful caps and cloaks seem strange and jolly in this ugly place.

A cold wind blows on us from our exposed position. Cranmer leans over and looks keenly at the pyre and at the crowd. He holds out a shaking hand as if to touch his friends. His lips move but I do not know what he is saying. Then I see the procession of people that surround Ridley and Latimer as they walk through the North Gate, Latimer lagging behind. Their white heads are bare. Some women from the crowd shower blessings on them. Others shout these down, and yell abuse at the prisoners.

The men are led to the pile of wood. Their clothes are stripped from them and replaced by long shirts daubed with sulphur. A bag of gunpowder is hung around Ridley's neck. They are chained to the stake, back to back. I see them speak to each other. For over two hours Dr Smith preaches the sermon. When he is finished there is some discussion with Lord Williams. As sometimes happens, he may be offering them a final chance to recant so that they might be spared. It seems they refuse as the executioner lights the straw all around the circle, and then retreats outside it. The gap is closed with more wood and the fire begins to take hold. The men turn their faces to the heavens and pray out loud.

The gorse bursts into flame and smoke billows in the wind. The gawking crowd goes quiet, all eyes fixed on the fire. Then from behind cries can be heard. I hear them asking God to receive their spirits, and I offer my own pleas for them.

A few people in the crowd start singing the Protestant hymn *A Mighty Fortress is Our God*, but they are hushed by their friends. Ridley cries out in agony. Suddenly a man breaks free of the cordon and throws more kindling on his side to speed up the process so that he might die sooner. The man is dragged away and pushed into the crowd.

As the wind is blowing in our direction the smell of smoke and burning flesh reaches us. I gag and swallow. Cranmer turns his head to either side looking for escape, but we form a solid wall behind him. Then he collapses sideways and I catch him and put him standing again, feeling his thin arms through his cloak.

The flames cover the pyre and lick their way up the stake. Sometimes the wind parts them and the men can be seen, their clothes burned away, the fire taking hold on their bare bodies. Latimer is almost covered in flames but his head hangs down. He has lost consciousness. Ridley is not so lucky. The extra wood has dampened the fire and his legs are being consumed slowly. He cries out to God for mercy. One of the men-at-arms pulls some faggots away with his bill and the flames rise up again on Ridley's body. They reach the bag of gunpowder and it explodes. At last he dies.

After nearly an hour the remains hang from the chains, black and burning like torches. The people, as if suddenly ashamed, filter slowly away from the scene.

'Take him back,' the governor orders and we help

Cranmer, who is barely able to walk, to his cell. We sit him on the cot and leave him, his head bowed. I lock the door and wait for the others to go down the steps. Then I rush around the corner and vomit on the floor.

For the rest of the day the prison is quieter than usual. Even the debtors do not plead aloud as they lower the collection cup to receive alms from people passing under the arch. I pace up and down, more aware than ever before of the torment of the man behind the door.

At last evening comes and I leave the prison and go to The Catherine Wheel. It is packed with men of every kind. Most have been drinking since after the burnings and are loud and careless. They shout and argue with each other. I do not see anyone I know and I do not wish to speak to strangers. Finding a stool to sit on, I drink a jug of ale and wait for numbness to come.

The conversation around me is of the executions. Not of how brave and steadfast the men were, not of the strength of their belief in Protestant principles that they would die for them. They talk only of the burnings, how much smoke the fire produced, how the weather was fair, and who stayed to the end. They speak of Ridley's slow death, and even laugh at his brother-in-law's attempt to shorten his suffering, which prolonged his agony instead.

I leave this company and go home. My mother is on her knees praying. She gets up and looks at me. I remove my cap and try to wash the sticky smoke from my head and face. She passes me bread and a bowl of soup. I sit and eat. Sitting opposite, she watches me.

'At least you did not have to be there this time,' she says.

'I did. Queen Mary gave instruction that Cranmer was to witness it.'

She puts her hand to her mouth holding in her breath.

'We had a better view than anyone. On the North Gate Tower.'

'Oh, Yon,' she says.

I want to tell her about the long sermon and Ridley's terrible suffering.

'They were so brave … it was so cruel…' I cannot go on. I chew and swallow. She remains silent.

'I just want to sleep now, Mother. I need to sleep,' I say, going to my cot.

'Yes, Yon.'

She gets up and hauls ash over the remaining embers. She bolts and bars the door. Then she dips her hand in the holy water and blesses herself as she goes to her room.

After that day I am more concerned about my prisoner. He refuses food and I hear him pacing the floor and praying aloud in a distressed voice. It is two years since he was condemned to death for treason, and condemned again in October last year for heresy. Having witnessed his friends suffering, I can only imagine the terror he endures as he awaits his own execution.

In the town there is much alarm at the burning of the two Protestant bishops and Queen Mary is losing some of the support she had when she became Queen. I, at least, have some peace, as my mother seems to have grown weary of her own bitterness in the face of what is happening around her. As time goes on she turns more into herself. She talks less and prays more.

Over the next six weeks, Cranmer has more visitors than before. His secretary and the Dean of Christchurch visit often. Members of Queen Mary's Privy Council come in their black full-length robes, fur stoles and black hats. They hold their noses as they come down the passageway. One of them speaks very urgently saying, 'We must persuade him to recant fully. He cannot meet his end like the others.'

I hear in early December Rome has decreed that he is not an Archbishop any more. A few days later Will and I are instructed to take him to the Dean's house in the

University, and for me to guard outside as he is still a prisoner. We go by the place where I had heard Father Latimer preach about the Catholic practices, and how they were designed by Rome to control and hold power over us. He made me think about the rites and rituals ordered by the Vatican and the many rules that came from the Pope. The priests made them seem more important than faith itself. I wondered about so much guidance from afar when all we need is to follow instruction from the Bible.

We arrive at the Dean's house where Cranmer is warmly greeted. I stand in my position outside and take stock of my surroundings. There is an archway, which shelters me from the elements, and I can see access to the quarters from all sides. I breathe in the fresh air and thank God for the change.

For two months he remains there and his friends, the Privy Council members and the Spanish friars they call Garcina and Roscius, visit him often.

One evening he is alone and asks me inside. Surprised, I hesitate at first, and then go in. He leads me into a timber-panelled room with a stone fireplace filled with blazing logs. There is a large table with leather-backed chairs in front of it. He gives me a drink of mead.

'Thank you, My Lord.'

'You do not need to address me so. I have been degraded from Holy Orders. They have taken my titles from me. I am a civilian like you now.' He turns to me, 'Can you read?'

'Yes, Master Cranmer.'

He goes to the table. It is covered with books and manuscripts. Among them *The Homilies* and *The Thirty-Nine Articles*. I also recognize *The Book of Common Prayer* we used in church. He waves his hand over them and says, 'This is my life's work.'

Then he sits on a chair, puts his hand on his chest and fingers the hair of his beard. His dark eyes are hooded with age, his face thin and his once tall frame curved over.

'My colleagues and I are responsible for much change. Now it is being swept aside as if it never happened, and I am expected to agree with that.'

I say nothing. I do not know why he is speaking to me like this.

He looks up at me and says, 'You are a young man. Are you happy to go back to the old ways? To be under Roman rule?'

I hesitate.

'You have nothing to fear from answering honestly. I will not betray you.'

'My family and I have suffered from the changes. We were tenants on the monastery land.'

He takes a deep breath and nods his head slowly.

'But I myself do not want to go back. I believe the new way is better,' I continue. He looks at me for a moment.

'You do not say this to comfort an old man?'

I answer firmly, 'No.'

'And your family?'

I look down at my boots. 'My mother is happy to have a Catholic Queen.'

'Understandable. And others in your family?'

'My father and brother died of the coughing disease when we moved into the town.'

'I am sorry. Such a loss.'

His face shows real sympathy. We are both silent. I am uncomfortable and the heat from the fire makes me sweat.

'Thank you, Master Cranmer.'

'Thank you, Yon.'

I try to walk lightly in my heavy boots across the polished floor. I take up my post outside again, glad of the December breeze, and wonder at the strange conversation.

A few months later I am instructed to bring him back to Bocardo. He stops at the familiar door and sighs.

'Here we are again, Yon,' he says quietly.

'Can I get you anything, Master Cranmer?' I ask, feeling sorry for him.

He shakes his head, shuffles to the chair and sits down. 'Only God can help me now.'

I close the door and lock it.

The winter months pass without change except for the many visits of the friar Juan de Garcina and members of the Council. They bring books. They leave with parchments.

In mid-March Dr Cole arrives from London. He visits Cranmer several times. After one of these visits Cole and the friars are very animated as they leave. It appears they have received a full recantation from him. The following day the friars arrive to take him to St Mary's Church where a sermon is to be preached by Dr Cole, and a statement to be read by Cranmer afterwards. The three leave together. As he passes me he turns and takes my free hand.

'God bless you, Yon. You have been kind. Thank you.'

'God bless you, Master Cranmer.'

Four of us have been told to go with them. As we leave the main gate I can hear the church bells ringing. It is raining as we make our way walking, the friars on either side of him. There are people all along the route. I see his mouth is open and his breath comes quickly. He walks carefully, looking mostly at the ground, and with his hands held out in front of him as if he couldn't see. Everyone knows who he is and some try to speak to him. We push them back so that he is not overwhelmed.

As we near St Mary's the crowd around it is loud and bold. There is an air of celebration. People mill around as if in the market place. Many smile and speak excitedly. Others wear grim faces. The souvenir sellers, which I have not seen since I was a small boy, have set up their stalls hung with scapulars, rosaries and images of the Virgin and Saints. Money changes hands. A priest stands on a box and preaches loudly about the fires of hell.

When we approach the church people are streaming into it. We take Cranmer to the back entrance through the convocation house and into the vestry. Members of the Privy Council meet and talk briefly to him. When a signal is given we lead him to a small raised dais by the pillar opposite the pulpit. He mounts it and stands there, looking around. The bells have stopped ringing and a surge of conversation can be heard.

The front pews are full with senior church members, the Mayor, Vice-Chancellor and Councilmen. Lord Williams is there also with many men-at-arms. Wealthy merchants and noblemen fill the pews behind them dressed in their colourful beaded garments of fine wools and satins. The peasants jostle and settle down, filling every corner of the small church. Dr Cole mounts the pulpit and gives a long sermon in which he speaks of the burnings of Protestants and Catholics going back to Henry's time and leading up to today's events.

When he is finished Cranmer begins to speak. His voice is strong despite his weak appearance, and his words clear. He begins by advising us not to get attached to this world, that we should work only towards the world to come. He entreats us to obey our Queen, as she is a minister of God. To love each other as brother and sister no matter what our beliefs and do no harm. He looks then at the wealthy in the front rows and asks them to consider scripture and be charitable to the poor, that giving to the poor is giving to God. Some of them shift a little and others whisper to each other, while the peasants behind them murmur.

As he speaks I notice a small bird flying around in the roof timbers. It dips and rises around the arches. Then it lands on the bottom of a high window in the nave, flying from pane to pane, its frail body fluttering against the coloured saints. Cranmer has stopped speaking. Suddenly the bird dives across the church, crashes against the opposite window and falls to the floor in the middle of the crowd. Cranmer looks down at his hands for a moment and then continues.

He talks of his conscience. Of the things he has written lately. He says that these later words are contrary to what he believes in his heart. There is a communal gasp and then silence. The council members look at each other and back at him again. He goes on to say he wrote the recantations only in fear of death and to save his life. He holds his writing hand up and says his recent writing is all untrue, and if he is to die let the hand that had betrayed his heart be burnt first.

The council are on their feet asking him to consider what he is saying. There is general uproar and people begin to move about. Lord Williams gives orders to his men-at-arms. They surround Cranmer. He continues to speak in a louder voice. He says that the Pope is our enemy, that he is an Antichrist and that his doctrine is false. Cranmer is pulled from the dais. There is bedlam in the church as we push through to get him outside.

'Take him to the stake,' Lord Williams shouts. The men-at-arms half drag, half walk him down the street. Riders on horseback join us to make way. We turn out the North Gate and stop at the stake. As they remove his cap and cloak, his eyes meet mine briefly. He looks calmer and happier than I have ever seen him. I long to tell him that I am with him in heart, that his life's work is the truth and will live forever. But I cannot.

He is roughly tied to the stake, the executioner lights the straw and closes the circle. We form a cordon as close as we dare. The fire takes hold and blazes fiercely. Cranmer prays aloud as he holds his hand out into the fire and keeps it there. He does not cry out. I pray like I have never prayed before for God to take him quickly. Through the raging wall of heat I can still see his outstretched hand. Then it is gone. The fire crackles and roars around the stake but there is still no sound from its wretched victim.

The crowd is still and quiet. We watch and wait. After a short time the executioner pronounces him dead.

I look up to Heaven and plead that he may be the last to suffer this terrible ordeal, and pray that Christ is taking him into His Kingdom.

THE FALL OF MANY

BY STELLA LANIGAN

Thomas knew that if the Parliamentarians were to secure victory this storm could not fail. The Royalists were steadfast in their disposition to control the town. Battles had been won and lost elsewhere but this siege had divided the people of Colchester with unease. A ban on trading left the town distressed. Horse meat became a source of food for humans. Inhabitants who could leave did but many of the poor had perished through disease, hunger or in support of their King. Now nearing the end of August, death was destined for the remainder if a treaty could not be entered into soon. Back at camp, men had nearly ten weeks with little food, less sleep and no pay, leaving them tired and weary. Tempers were beginning to take hold.

'We're ready,' John said, coming to stand beside Thomas. 'They're just awaiting instruction.'

'Tell them when I raise my hand it will be my signal,' Thomas replied.

Hunching down behind the trenched stone wall, Thomas knew this could be his last night as a free man if Fairfax's plan did not work. Raising his hand, Thomas heard the quiver in his own voice as he shouted, 'Fire!'

The shot from the cannon sent a strident roar from the men as they made charge in great fury on the enemy line. The cannonball struck the belly of the wall at St Mary's, causing the ground to quake. Stones started to spit from the dust, hitting some of the men and beating them back to the ground. The Royal Regiment began to scurry and run for cover as the walls of St Mary's came tumbling down, bringing with them the large culverin that had been planted on the top of the tower. Chaos descended upon the High

Street. Knowing that his job was done, Thomas called John.

'Direct the men to return to camp or seek safety of some sort,' he ordered. 'When Lucas realises the impact of this blast, it's only a matter of time before all the King's horses and all the King's men are sent out in search of prisoners.'

'Where are you going?' John asked.

'I must seek out the whereabouts of my sister and ensure her safe passage.'

'You can always send her to Willow's Gap. She will be well cared for there.'

'Thank you, John. God speed.' Thomas turned swiftly and headed for home.

Lizzie felt the shake as the walls of St Mary's crumbled to the ground. Tin plates and cups fell to the floor with a clatter. Thomas's entry through the front door meant Lizzie's prayers were answered.

'Thank God you're safe,' Lizzie said. 'What's happening?'

'No time, we have to hurry,' Thomas replied.

Taking Lizzie by the arm, Thomas ushered her out the door. Clouds of dust filled the air, blurring her vision, filtering their way into the lining of her throat and causing her to start coughing.

'Here, cover your nose and mouth with this.' Thomas handed Lizzie a handkerchief. 'We don't want attention drawn to us. Keep your head down and quicken your pace.'

'Where are we going?'

'Willow's Gap.'

'Willow's Gap? But that's miles away.'

'If they find me, Lizzie, my head will be in the hands of the Hangman.'

The cobblestones stung Lizzie's feet as she hurried alongside Thomas. The closer they got to the Green at St

John's, the more the streets filled up with anxious townspeople heading in the opposite direction. Many were howling and crying in anguish, hoping for some compassion, others stumbling from street to street oppressed. Suddenly there was another loud bang and everyone began charging back down the way in which they came. Thomas steered Lizzie in the direction of Suffolk Road. Bouncing down the steps, they cut through Archers Lane heading towards Eastern Bridge. On hearing the sounds of a regiment, Thomas slowed his step to get a sense of their approach.

'Hush.' Thomas extended his arm to halt Lizzie.

'What is it?' Lizzie asked.

'Wait here.' Thomas pushed her into the doorway of the old mill. 'I'll be back shortly.'

'You can't go and leave me here!'

'It's safer if you stay here while I check something. I'll be back.'

'But what if you're not?'

'If I'm not, make your way to Willow's Gap and look for the house of Jack Smyth.'

'Jack Smyth. Who is he? Where will I find him?' But before she knew it Thomas had disappeared back up the steps, leaving Lizzie alone in one of the few empty streets of Colchester.

Almost afraid to breathe for fear of being found, Lizzie tucked herself in the doorway and stood silent. In the distance she heard the pleas and protests of people who were being beaten. Soon the shouts and screams were getting nearer and she knew she could not stay there much longer or she would be found. She prayed once again for Thomas's safe return and went to move from the doorway when she was suddenly caught from behind. Someone was forcefully pushing her to the ground.

'What have we got here?' A man had a tight grip on her hair. Her struggles to break free seemed to heighten his laughter, causing his sturdy frame to move back and forth even more.

'Is it a wee wench I see?' He turned Lizzie to face him. Lizzie began kicking and screaming. His jaw was pockmarked and his breath smelt of stale whisky and tobacco, combined with a musty uniform, causing Lizzie's stomach to feel nauseous.

'What's the matter lass? Not used to being in the presence of Royalty?' The soldier forced a tighter grip on her neck. 'Now what has you out here all alone?'

Lizzie's mouth felt dry and, even if she wanted to speak, the words just wouldn't come out.

Leaning his square-shaped body in on hers, he said, 'Cat got your tongue?' He ran his rough hand round Lizzie's throat and down her bosom. 'You smell nice.'

'Freeman! What the hell are you doing?' roared a man running down the street.

'Just doing my duty, sir.' The soldier released Lizzie and let her fall to the ground. 'Checking out the streets like you asked.'

'Since when is it the duty of a foot soldier to harass a servant of the King's court? Get back to your infantry at once.'

Freeman straightened the scabbard around his waist before rubbing the sweat from his brow, then eyed Lizzie up and down.

'Whatever you say, sir.' He walked away.

'Let me help you.' The Sergeant extended a hand to Lizzie. 'I apologise for the behaviour of one of my footmen.'

'Thank you,' Lizzie replied.

'If I may say so, this is no place for a young lady. Why aren't you heading in the direction of the courthouse like everyone else as instructed?'

'I was just going to check on my aunt.' Lizzie straightened out her dress, avoiding his eyes.

'And where would your aunt live?'

'Over by Eastern Bridge.'

'Not the safest of places to be visiting with blockades everywhere.'

'Well that could be said for many parts of England at present.'

'Perhaps,' the Sergeant replied. 'But aside from the present siege in which we find ourselves, is it not true that the area known as Eastern Bridge is housed with thieves, traitors and bigots?'

'That depends on one's interpretation of them.' Lizzie turned to walk away.

'Does it now?' The Sergeant stepped in front of her path. 'Would you care to enlighten me somewhat as to your definition then?'

'The people whom you call thieves are deprived daily of the basic right to food and shelter but are still expected to pay dues and taxes to your so-called King who has no notion of hardship and no knowing of the struggles that face his people. So if one must use thievery to feed his family then it is the laws that govern these lands which are wrong and not the thief.'

The Sergeant stood silent.

'Thank you for your assistance.' Lizzie turned and ran down the street towards Eastern Bridge.

It was late evening when Lizzie finally made her way to Willow's Gap. Exhausted, she enquired at the blacksmith's as to where Jack Smyth might be found.

'Jack Smyth is a hard man to track down,' the blacksmith replied, 'but for a damsel like yourself I'm sure he'll make an exception.'

'I'm here on business.'

'Hmm! I bet you are.' The blacksmith chuckled.

'Please, sir, time is short. If you could just point me in his direction, I'll be on my way.'

'Unfortunately, time is short for all of us, lass. Go down that street there.' He pointed. 'When you hit on Hangman's Inn take a left. Follow the path till you come to the green split door. Enquire there.'

'Thank you kindly, sir,' Lizzie replied.

The man tilted his head, then began hammering a horse shoe on the anvil.

Lizzie's knocking sent a scurry of whispers and muffled voices inside the house. After a few moments had passed the latch was lifted. An elderly woman of stocky build, with a hint of silver running through her hair, opened the door and stood staring at Lizzie.

'I'm sorry for bothering you, ma'am, but would you know where I might find Jack Smyth?'

'Who's asking?'

'Oh! So sorry for my lack of manners,' Lizzie replied. 'Elizabeth Edwards – Lizzie for short.' She extended her hand.

Rubbing both hands in her apron, the woman broadened the door.

'We're not used to formalities round these parts,' the woman said. 'You'd better come in before someone sees. We've been expecting you.'

'The men are disheartened, sir.' Thomas sat with Fairfax around the camp fire in Lexden.

'Victory is in sight. You must keep them engaged,' Fairfax said.

'They are honourable to the cause but with so many men lost in battle, their fear is victory will come too late for them.'

'Many of our battles are already won. Surely they must see the victory in that? More forces are already dispatched from London and Suffolk. Fresh men and horses. It is only a matter of time before Goring consents to the conditions of our treaty and our biggest battle to date will be won.'

'The blockade, sir. It has crippled the town. Many of the ordinary folk are hurt or have perished and the rest are struggling to survive. Our own are suffering just as much as the enemy. Surely we could show some compassion? This siege has negatively impacted on the spirits of the men. If we lift the ban on trading and allow some supplies?'

'Those in town chose their fate when they chose to follow their King. To allow trade in a town besieged would show weakness. I will not agree,' Fairfax replied.

'If you see it from their point of view, many still have family and friends who inhabit the town. These people did not choose their fate, war did through their circumstance and situation of employment. For some it was their only means to feed their families. Where were they to go? Some have not known life other than Colchester.'

'This siege has scorned many families but I will not consent to trading. Our strength is in knowing that the enemy is reduced in numbers and soon the King's men will have to lay down arms and surrender. You have fought hard, Thomas, so you need have no fear. You will be rewarded.'

'I seek only to ensure that the ordinary people of these lands have fair and equal rights,' Thomas replied.

'That is the right of all mankind, Thomas. Let us rest now and not use all our strength in talking.'

Another charge on the town of Colchester was about to be made the following day when a messenger sent word to the camp that the Royalists were laying down arms and would surrender.

'Who'd have thought, Thomas?' John said. 'We have succeeded in victory and survived.'

'I fear I am not as elated as you with the result,' Thomas replied.

'But surely you see the benefits to victory now?' John continued. 'The Parliamentarians have proven their purpose and right to influence within Government.'

'That is true, John, but at what price? There is a trail of bloodshed and destruction across England and it is as much the result of our hand as any Royalist.' Thomas placed his hand on John's shoulder. 'I must take leave of you now.' He mounted his horse.

'Where are you going?'

'I have to make haste to London if I am to stop further carnage of this kind.'

LITTLE STAR

BY RACHEL NOLAN

Rosie could hear the muffled laughter behind their hands as they waited for her to speak. The back of her shirt felt wet and her palms sticky.

'Twinkle, twinkle – come on Rosie, you know the words.'

She raised her head and gave her teacher, Sarah Murphy, a look that pleaded for mercy. In her head Rosie could hear the rhyme she'd practised endlessly. She'd said it for hours last night, slowly repeating it until her mouth felt dry and the words lost their meaning. She could feel the word forming: a bubble caught between her tongue and her teeth. She knew how to sound it out, to spell it, how to say it in her head. She tried to force it out quickly as she had done so many times before, but the word 'twinkle' stuck like tar to the roof of her mouth.

Twinkle, Twinkle, Little Star was Rosie's favourite nursery rhyme. The only memory she had of her mother. It took her a long time to remember all the words properly and longer to say them all the right way. But she knew them. The same way she knew her mother, the same way she would always know her mother. The clock ticked on the wall above her teacher's head, and the space between them grew heavier and darker with each second she kept Rosie sitting in the rotten silence. She wanted to cry. She tried one more time.

'T … t…' She breathed in deeply. 'T … t…'

She looked up and could see the words forming on her teacher's lips.

'Twinkle, twinkle, little star,' Claire O'Mahoney said defiantly, before sniggering into her hands.

'That's enough, Claire.'

Rosie looked at Claire's smirking face and felt her throat tighten with the effort of holding on to her shame. Claire sniggered again but more quietly and from the safety of her cupped hands this time.

Sarah Murphy sighed heavily and sat on her chair. Rosie had been in her class now for the last four months. Her speech showed no signs of improving but her homework was always done neatly and correctly. She had often observed her from afar with the other children, fearing that perhaps she unconsciously singled her out because she knew things about Rosie she wished she didn't. But over time she realised that Rosie Cleary was simply an interesting child. Kind, delicate yet effervescent, commanding fairness from the world that wasn't readily available.

Sarah didn't like Claire O'Mahoney. She was a bully. A wiry, demanding child who spent too much time with adults and not enough time having fun. Try as she might to antagonise Rosie it never worked. She just ignored Claire's attempts to dominate, yet any sniff of mutiny by the others was met with Rosie's scorn and aversion. Once Sarah even overheard Rosie reprimand another girl who tried to talk badly about Claire.

'Don't say things like that about her, that's not nice.'

'But Rosie, she said mean things about you and where you live.'

'I know but how do we know what *her* family is really like?'

This was all she would ever need to know about Rosie. A glimpse of a mighty person cocooned inside a shell of trapped words. But Rosie would go white every time Sarah asked her to speak in front of the class. That look of ferocious panic mixed with fear and resentment always found its target in Sarah. And she couldn't ask her not to speak, couldn't show any favouritism – the other children could sense a distinction like that. So many times she wanted to reach across the classroom and pull the words out for her, lean over and tenderly peel away each sentence layer by layer until there was a space for her to feel heard. A little girl without a voice would become a woman with a lot to say.

Most days Rosie had a pain in her tummy thinking about speaking in school the next day. Her evenings would be spent practising her words and rehearsing other ways to say things using words that were easier for her to say. She had trouble sleeping, running to the bathroom every time she thought about the different ways she might be laughed at for saying things wrong. It wasn't their sniggers that hurt so much as the sadness she felt because she knew the words, could say them right when no one was looking. But nobody could ever see that. The burning sensation was always there in her tummy at school, especially on Tuesdays. Tuesday was the day the priest came to the school. The family she lived with did not go to Mass on Sundays and she was always terrified that the priest would know this about her.

Tuesday mornings always came around faster than any other day and on this particular cold and wet January morning, when Rosie walked into the classroom, the priest was already sitting, waiting. Solemn and foreboding, he gave a slow nod for each child who walked in. Rosie was going to be asked this morning. She could feel it hanging over her, a feeling she had grown to remember. She would not be able to say a single word properly to the priest, this she knew with complete certainty and her whole class would go utterly silent waiting for her not to be able to say it.

'You there.' Rosie kept her head down. 'You, with the glasses and curls?'

Rosie's breath came in short, sharp bursts. She didn't look up. If she did, it would be real.

'Rosie Cleary, Fr Byrne is talking to you,' she heard

Sarah say in a foggy voice. She waited.

'Rosie?' Fr Byrne said. 'Give me a little smile then won't you?'

She didn't like the way he said those words, it was mean. She forced herself to look up. On his face he wore a smile but it didn't match the look in his eyes. She could feel the stickiness of her palms as she clutched her hands together under the table.

'Now, Rosie, can you tell me what the Gospel was about on Sunday?'

Everything in her head went white and she had to use the bathroom so urgently that she crossed her legs. She knew so few names from the Bible and the easiest one she could say was Mark. If it was wrong the whole class would laugh and the priest would know she hadn't been to Mass. If she couldn't say it right they would laugh harder. She could feel his eyes on her, everyone waiting; she was repeating Mark over and over in her head. It was there. She could feel it fizzing on her tongue, her mouth was slightly open and she was trying to push it out of the bubble.

'God,' she said breathless, 'it was about God.'

Laughter bounced around the room. Rosie sat back in her chair and clenched her bum to try and stop the flow of pee that had started to run into her tights.

'You've quite the comedian here, Miss Murphy.' He sized Rosie up over his glasses. 'Are you the young girl staying with the Donnellys?' he asked slowly.

'Yes,' Rosie said in a whisper.

'What did you say? Speak up, let God hear you.' His voice made several children jump.

'Father, will you have some tea?' Sarah asked.

He dismissed her with his hand and asked again. 'Are you the young girl staying with the Donnellys?'

'Yes,' she said a little louder. Someone coughed.

'Are they treating you nice?'

'Yes,' she spoke softly and kept her head down.

'I don't see them at Mass; do they go to Mass on Sundays?'

'Some…' she breathed in and tried again. 'Some … sometimes.'

The priest smiled. 'Interesting. I've never seen them there.' He took off his glasses and wiped them with his shirt. 'Maybe I should get you to read a bit of the Gospel for us all to hear it … Rosie … what do you think?'

'Father, will you not have a drop of tea on such a cold morning?' Sarah said quickly, 'I believe we have some of your favourite biscuits too.'

He put his glasses back on and peered out over them. 'I suppose I could. Rosie, I'll look forward to our next little chat. Maybe you might read a bit for me then.'

Rosie nodded and could feel the warm fear as it trickled down her legs.

Sarah saw the look of triumph on the priest's face. He had done it for sport. Rosie's face told her the same. The shame, the guilt, that silent insidious thinking had been given a pulse. Rosie had been defeated at a game she was too young yet to play. It was a ruthless thing to do, but for Sarah it too was a reality she had uncovered earlier than she was ready to explore. This awareness was not slow, but a quick authenticity that stole treasures she could only appreciate the measure of now. She hated him so fiercely in that moment, but she hated herself more for not having the nerve to quieten Fr Byrne before Rosie felt the full impact of his intentions.

She opened the classroom door and stood back to let Fr Byrne out. She turned and asked the class to try and make as little noise as possible while she made him some tea. The thick, tense air was slowly seeping through the cracks in the old walls. As she closed the door behind her, Sarah looked across to Rosie. She sat with her head in her hands and Sarah's heart almost snapped in half at the sight of her.

Rosie kept her head down until the noise in the classroom grew a little heavier and people moved across to their friends. She didn't want to risk moving from her chair yet. She looked up and caught Claire looking at her. She smiled a little but Rosie didn't care. She was trying so hard to swallow the dry, salty lump in her throat. She looked around at the others and wondered did they know the things she knew, feel the things she felt. Sometimes Rosie would stare at herself in the mirror for so long, trying to see traces of a person she could barely remember, that she seldom even recognised the face staring back.

She could hear plans for a birthday party underway at Claire's table. The other girls in her class did not often invite her to their houses. If they did they asked her hundreds of questions she didn't want to answer. She would usually just smile and say that it was just this way for now but it wouldn't be this way always, knowing in her heart that nothing was ever for always. Rosie never grew too attached to anything because it could and would be just another thing she would have to feel sad about. She didn't need any other reasons for that.

Sarah led Fr Byrne into the staff room. On remembering that there were good biscuits in the tin she was instantly annoyed. Fr Byrne would protest as usual about not wanting to eat them because of his cholesterol but on her second offer he would proceed to eat half a packet of chocolate Hobnobs, washed down with two cups of tea so weak it was almost watered milk. Then he would make his rounds to the other classes before making his way back for Mass at half eleven. Having been brought up by parents who believed that good manners, hard work, diligence and compassion led to respect, she found this enforced civility towards Fr Byrne infuriating. Sarah was pouring the second cup of tea when Fr Byrne asked her about Rosie.

'That girl Rosie – do we know much about her?'

'What do you mean?' Sarah asked, fearing his reply. 'I know as much as I should – being her teacher.'

'Oh I know, I know, but it's a very strange set up altogether.'

'How so?'

'Oh, the Donnellys are nice enough people.'

Sarah turned to put the milk into the fridge and threw her eyes up to Heaven.

'It's almost half ten, Father. Maybe you ought to stop into the other classes before Mass. Couldn't have you late.' She smiled.

'Oh, is that the time?'

As he got up from the chair Sarah could hear the cracks and groans of both the chair and the man. It was a sound she was familiar with but she couldn't quite place it. It reminded her of a feeling that she once had. It moved around in her body like a cold wave and was released with a loud sigh. She could feel Fr Byrne's hand on her shoulder as he asked if she was ok.

'Sorry, Father. I didn't have breakfast and I felt a bit faint. I'm ok now.'

'Well, if you're sure.' He opened the door. 'See you soon, Miss Murphy,' he said, as he walked out.

Sarah quietly made her way back to her classroom. The children's chatter turned to loud whispers as she walked in. She looked around but Rosie was gone. She walked down to her desk and asked if anyone had seen her. They all shrugged. When Sarah looked down at Rosie's chair she noticed the damp patch; she pushed it under the table. Deep inside her something started ticking and she prayed that no one had seen the seat. She told Claire to sit at the top of the classroom and keep the others quiet while she did something important.

Walking towards the bathroom she could hear a tap going full force and when she opened the door Rosie stood there with her tights in her hand.

'Is everything ok in here, Rosie?'

She looked startled to see Sarah in the bathroom.

'Eh … yes Miss … Mur … Mu … Mmm … yes, Miss. I spilled something.'

'I'm sorry that happened, Rosie, would you like some help?'

'No … thank you, it's ok.'

'I don't go to Mass either Rosie,' she offered.

Rosie looked up with eyes that didn't believe her.

'Miss … do you think Heaven is real?'

Sarah looked down at her. Barefoot, raw and exposed, and for the first time in her life really wishing she could say yes and mean it.

'Honestly Rosie, I don't know. What do you think?' She watched as Rosie's face twisted into an expression she couldn't quite read.

'Miss … I can't answer that.'

'Why not Rosie? I won't tell anyone. It will be our secret.'

Rosie's face hardened.

'Even God has secrets, Rosie.' Sarah reached over to take the tights from her hands.

Rosie started to cry then. Soft, heavy drops left their mark on her shirt.

'Do you think God can keep them all?' Rosie whispered softly, wiping her eyes.

Sarah looked at Rosie, beautiful in her innocence, waiting for so much but asking for so little. Sarah held the tights, soaked in all the words Rosie would never be able to say, under the dryer. They both stood with only the soft hum of the dryer breaking the silence between them. After a while Rosie reached up, took the damp tights out of Sarah's hand and put them back on. When she was done she opened the door and stepped into the long corridor. As she walked away, shoes in her hands, Sarah saw the prints of her damp feet on the cold tiles. The sun coming in the window dried them up just as quickly as she made them.

Its opaque light beamed into the long corridor and lit up Rosie until she was almost translucent. She turned and faced Sarah.

'Twinkle, twinkle, little star,' Rosie said and smiled shyly. Then she opened the classroom door, the darkness swallowed her, and she was gone.

DR FOSTER'S PATIENCE PAYS OFF

BY VALERIE RYAN

'Doctor Foster went to Gloucester…' Mrs Barrett chanted the rhyme in a cross voice.

'That only applies to male Dr Fosters, obviously,' Cathy Foster laughed as she spoke, and gripped either side of the stethoscope that hung over her white coat. She had checked Mrs Barrett's heart rate and was pleased with what she heard.

'Have you been to Gloucester?' Violet Barrett pointed at Cathy from her bed and added, 'Where's my money?'

'No. Mrs Barrett, I haven't been to Gloucester and I didn't take your money. You spent it on champagne and furs. Remember? That's what you told me yesterday.'

'I'm so sorry, my dear.' Her patient's expression changed to confusion and then cleared. Her hand went to her forehead. 'I don't know why I said that, I don't know what's wrong with me. I'm just a silly old woman.'

'You have an infection and it's making you feel strange. That's all. And you're never silly, you're a wonderful woman. If I live to ninety-four, I hope I'm like you.'

'Are you working again tomorrow?'

'I'm…,' Cathy glanced down at her watch, '…finished … now.' She wrote a note on the chart, clipped it back to the end of the bed, and sat down on the bedside stool. 'I won't see you again, I'm off for a week. You'll be right as rain and back home by the time my holiday is over. Don't worry, I'm not going to Gloucester in this chilly spring weather.' She laughed.

'I will miss you, my dear. I'm sorry I say silly things. Mind you,' Mrs Barrett patted Cathy's hand, 'I did once know a Dr Foster who wished he were far away from anywhere.' She spoke in a low voice.

'Oh, tell me more.' The doctor leant nearer the bed. Listening to her elderly patients ramble on was a welcome distraction.

Her patient fussed with the pink bow on her bed jacket and glanced out the window a moment.

'Bill Foster. His mother called him Billy. He did a few years in medical school and got some kind of licentiate, whatever it was – it was enough for him to put up a plate.' She stopped a moment and frowned. 'What was I saying, my dear?'

'Bill Foster. Take your time,' Cathy said in a soothing voice.

'Yes. I remember now. Billy took fancy consulting rooms in one of the Georgian buildings not far from the city centre. Quite a few steps up to the front door. Not much good if you were ill.'

'How did he do? Was he a good doctor?' Cathy lowered her voice, leant an elbow on the bed and rested on her hand.

'If you were worried but well, there was no one better. Perish the thought you might actually be sick. He soon had a reputation. He's long dead now so I don't mind telling you my sister worked for him.'

'What did he specialise in?'

Mrs Barrett glanced from left to right before she spoke, almost in a whisper. 'He specialised in … middle-aged women. Preferably rich ones with more money than sense. Usually they had a medical dictionary at home and diagnosed themselves as having terrible illnesses. Billy was the quack for them. Just so long as they weren't sick and were very grateful. I'm sorry my dear, I don't mean to speak ill of your colleagues, but he was a different kind of doctor to you.'

'Fascinating. Do go on.'

'He must have been there about, let me see, fifteen

years. The same patients were going to him all the time and were very well. My sister still swears he never had any affairs with those women but I don't know. He fancied himself no end. Of course, after fifteen years, some of those women started to become sick. They complained about the steps, some had heart problems and couldn't make the stairs. He thought he'd weed them out one by one and get new patients.'

'And did he?' Cathy asked.

'No. By then he couldn't hide his big tummy in fancy suits, and his lah-di-dah accent didn't bring them in the way it once did. He was soon in trouble with the banks.'

'Oh, was he a drinker? A gambler?'

Mrs Barrett looked blankly for a moment at Cathy and her brow furrowed. 'Who was I talking about?'

'Billy Foster. The doctor,' Cathy prompted.

'Oh yes. But,' she paused, 'the scoundrel didn't pay my sister her wages for three weeks. She couldn't wait any longer and got a job with a proper doctor across town. Billy had to get his mother in to answer the phone and the door, but only until one of his patients died,' she dropped her voice to a whisper, 'and left him fifty thousand pounds. A fortune.' She stared out the window and repeated, 'A fortune.'

'What happened then?'

'As you might expect, he was living the high life and got in a very slatternly young woman as a secretary. A refugee during the war from one of those Baltic countries. He told everyone it was a noble act to give her work. My sister was always a bitter girl. She said his new secretary was surely doing *different* work,' she whispered the word 'different' and nodded her head at Cathy, 'to the kind she had done while she was there.'

'Did you hear any more about the patient who died?'

'Eyebrows were raised when he got the money but she had no family and in those days, my dear, you could be as healthy as a horse and drop dead of flu the next day. Quite,

quite different to life now. Look how well you take care of me.'

'It's a pleasure. Are you saying he did away with a patient for her money?'

'No, dear.'

'That's a relief, I thought you meant he had done something to end her life?'

'No, my dear, he did away with three patients, not one.'

Cathy sat straight back from the bed in a sudden movement, with her elbow still crooked and looked at her patient. 'You know you're saying he murdered three people?'

'I do, dear, and I'm telling you the terrible truth. Mother will give out to me but it's about time someone said what happened. Those poor silly women.'

Cathy was about to remind her that 'Mother' was long dead but restrained herself.

'Somehow, the secretary, let me see, she's Russian? Did I tell you that already?'

'You did.'

'Good. Well, she managed to get past his mother and got him to marry her. My sister said she pretended she was in the family way. I doubt that, my dear, who better than him to dispense with that problem? No, I believe she knows his dirty secrets.'

'Knew...?' Dr Cathy Foster raised an eyebrow and spoke in a gentle voice.

'Yes, knew them.' Mrs Barrett spoke quickly, sounding troubled. 'The twins were his next victims. The 'flu, my eye. The Liverpool 'flu of '50 was long over and had taken its fair share of young and old, but this was the end of '51.'

'Who were the twins?' Cathy leant in.

'Alicia and Patricia. Everyone called them the Sha–s. Their mother barked at her daughters the whole time, 'Get my bag, –cia' or 'Give me my coat, –cia'. No one ever knew which one she was calling. Their daddy had left a fortune after the First World War. Horses.' She stopped and stared at Cathy a moment, appearing confused.

'Horses? Yes, do go on.'

'Where was I? Oh yes, he had sent every horse he could lay his hand on to the British Army and they sent them on to France. Mother was convinced some were donkeys. He bought that lovely old place you pass after the roundabout and planted all those trees you see at the front. And he made wise investments. After he was gone, the twins' mother reigned like the Queen – what am I saying?' Mrs Barrett's cheeks coloured and her voice cracked. Cathy offered her the glass of water from the bedside locker. She took a sip.

'What happened to their mother?' Cathy asked.

'Kept them like a pair of pet hens right up until the end.' She mimed as though she were throwing back a drink. 'They were forty-five by then and lost until they found Billy. They followed him around like lapdogs. No other family, you see.'

'But how could he have got away with such a thing?'

'His cousin. He was the coroner, Billy made sure he was called in. He signed off on their death certs. We guessed he smothered them or my sister also thought it might have been poison.'

'Oh, the coroner? His cousin? Why on earth would he?' Cathy sat up straight and gaped.

The old lady watched her a moment with her watery blue eyes, bright and focused. This time she mimed a gesture for money with her hand. 'He loved the gee-gees, my dear. The fool of a cousin was in a lot of trouble and since everyone knew the Sha–s would leave everything to Billy, he made sure the cousin smoothed over the details. But then of course, the bread you throw on the water comes back to you.' Mrs Barrett folded her hands, the age spots making them appear tanned.

'Back to you?' Cathy used an encouraging tone.

'Billy had a massive heart attack a year after the Sha–s died and what's-her-name was killed in a car accident.

They were the smallest funerals I've ever been at.'

'Who…?' Cathy stopped.

'Who got the fortune? From the dead patients? A grand nephew from near here. Another Foster. They had such notions. All cut from the same cloth. They'll have no luck with that money until they atone for the murders of those silly women.'

The doctor jerked her head up and her jaw dropped before she spoke in an abrupt tone. 'Nonsense. All coincidences. Malicious gossip. No doubt.' She grasped the stethoscope still around her neck and stood up. Her expression was taut and she stared a moment.

'If you say so. Dr Foster went to…,' Mrs Barrett started and stopped speaking, smiled up at her and folded her hands.

Cathy snatched up the chart again from the end of the bed and added another note: *Tuesday. 11 am. Vital signs normal. Brief cognitive assessment. Long-term recall distorted, imagined events appear real to patient.*

She said nothing but strode out of the room. There was a prolonged silence after the door closed before her steps sounded along the hall. Mrs Barrett settled back on her pillows and let out a small chuckle.

THE RHYMES

AND

THEIR BACKGROUNDS

Oranges and Lemons

Oranges and lemons, say the bells of St. Clement's.

You owe me five farthings, say the bells of St. Martin's.

When will you pay me? say the bells of Old Bailey.

When I grow rich, say the bells of Shoreditch.

When will that be? say the bells of Stepney.

I do not know, says the great bell of Bow.

Here comes a candle to light you to bed,

And here comes a chopper to chop off your head!

Chip, chop, chip, chop,

The last man's dead!

Possibly originating from a square dance called *Oranges and Lemons* dating back to 1665. The place names relate to current or previously existing churches in London and the tune to which the lyrics are sung can easily be imagined as the pealing of church bells.

Children playing the game of Oranges and Lemons end in a finale with the last child through an archway of upheld arms being caught, simulating the act of chopping off their head. The rhyme tells the story of someone in debt who is processed by the legal system of the time and meets a sticky end for their crimes. Perhaps one of the most sinister children's rhymes.

The story *The Oranges and Lemons Eulogy* by R.A. Barnes is inspired by this rhyme.

Sing a Song of Sixpence

Sing a song of sixpence, a pocket full of rye.

Four and twenty blackbirds, baked in a pie.

When the pie was opened, the birds began to sing;

Wasn't that a dainty dish, to set before the king?

The king was in his counting house, counting out his money;

The queen was in the parlour, eating bread and honey.

The maid was in the garden, hanging out the clothes,

When down came a blackbird and pecked off her nose.

This rhyme is believed to be a parody of the relationship between King Henry VIII of England and his second wife Anne Boleyn. It was not uncommon in the 16th century for a chef to hide surprises in a pie and blackbirds added novelty. The number 24 has been tied to the Reformation and the printing of the English Bible with 24 letters. From a folklore tradition, the blackbird taking the maid's nose has been seen as a demon stealing her soul. It is a rhyme laced with symbolism.

The story *Sing a Song of Sixpence* by Maura Barrett is inspired by this rhyme.

Hey Diddle Diddle

Hey diddle diddle, the cat and the fiddle,

The cow jumped over the moon.

The little dog laughed to see such fun,

And the dish ran away with the spoon!

There is much speculation and controversy over the origins of *Hey Diddle Diddle*, which is at heart a nonsense rhyme. Some claim it refers to Lady Katherine Grey and her relationships with the Earl of Hertford and the Earl of Leicester, others that it represents a variety of constellations. It has also been suggested that it might denote Katherine of Aragon (Katherine la Fidèle) or symbolize anti-clerical feeling following injunctions by Catholic priests for harder work. The name 'Cat and the Fiddle' was a common name for inns; one such inn existed at Old Chaunge, London by 1587.

The term 'Hey diddle diddle' can be found in writings by Shakespeare; it's likely the original title was 'High Diddle Diddle' but that this was altered over time as language usage changed. The first known publication for the words of the rhyme is 1765; by that stage, the rhyme may already have been in existence for two centuries as lines in a Thomas Preston play printed in 1569 mention:

'They be at hand Sir with stick and fiddle;

They can play a new dance call hey-didle-didle.'

Written in 1597, *The Cherry and the Slae* by Alexander Montgomerie, the Scottish Jacobean courtier and poet, also suggests the existence of the rhyme *Hey Diddle Diddle*:

> '*But since you think't an easy thing*
>
> *To mount above the moon,*
>
> *Of your own fiddle take a spring*
>
> *And dance when you have done.*'

The story *The Fiddle* by Jeanne Beary suggests how a rhyme such as this could be inspired by the retelling of a simple event. She sets her story in the modern day and re-interprets the incidents recounted in the rhyme.

There was a Crooked Man

There was a crooked man, and he walked a crooked mile.

He found a crooked sixpence upon a crooked stile.

He bought a crooked cat, which caught a crooked mouse,

And they all lived together in a little crooked house.

This traditional English nursery rhyme originates from the time of King Charles I (1600-1649). The 'crooked man' is reputed to be the Scottish General, Sir Alexander Leslie, who signed a covenant securing religious and political freedom for Scotland. The 'crooked stile' refers to the border between England and Scotland. The 'little crooked house' tells how the English and Scots eventually came to an agreement, despite the continuing animosity between them.

The remains of King Richard III of England, the last Plantagenet King, were discovered buried in a crude grave in a car park in Leicester, the original site of Greyfriars Friary Church, in September 2012, and proven beyond reasonable doubt on 4th February 2013.

The story *Restoration* by Ilona Blunden is inspired both by this rhyme and by the most significant archaeological discovery of recent times.

Mary had a Little Lamb

Mary had a little lamb, its fleece was white as snow;

And everywhere that Mary went, the lamb was sure to go.

It followed her to school one day, which was against the rule;

It made the children laugh and play, to see a lamb at school.

And so the teacher turned it out, but still it lingered near,

And waited patiently about, till Mary did appear.

While the author Phyllida Clarke has used a certain amount of artistic licence with her piece of fiction *The Sad Tale of Mary Sawyer's Little Lamb*, this is basically a true story as told by Mary Sawyer to a relative, Henry Sawyer, many years later and sworn before a Notary Public in Sterling, Massachusetts in 1901. It was recounted in a book *The Story of Mary's Little Lamb* published by Mr and Mrs Henry J. Ford in 1928.

It is unclear how the poem came into the hands of Sarah Jane Hale who first published it in a book of moralistic poems in 1830. Sarah Jane Hale was a well-known campaigner against slavery. She is credited with having added the final twelve lines:

And then he ran to her and laid

His head upon her arm,

As if he said - 'I'm not afraid -

You'll keep me from all harm.'

What makes the lamb love Mary so?

The eager children cry –

O Mary loves the lamb, you know,

The teacher did reply –

And you each gentle animal

In confidence may bind,

And make them follow at your call,

If you are always kind.

The poem became universally famous when it was the first words recorded by Thomas Edison on a piece of tin foil in 1878. In 1927 Edison remade this recording and it still survives.

Jack Sprat

Jack Sprat could eat no fat,

His wife could eat no lean,

And so betwixt the two of them

They licked the platter clean.

Jack ate all the lean,

Joan ate all the fat.

The bone they picked it clean,

Then gave it to the cat.

Jack Sprat was wheeling

His wife by the ditch.

The barrow turned over,

And in she did pitch.

Says Jack, 'She'll be drowned!'

But Joan did reply,

'I don't think I shall,

For the ditch is quite dry.'

The Jack Sprat of this English poem is alleged to be King Charles I (1600-1649) and Sprat's wife his Queen Henrietta Maria (1609-1669). When King Charles I (Jack Sprat) declared war on Spain, Parliament refused to finance the venture and so his wife subsequently imposed an illegal war tax. The angered King then dissolved Parliament.

The story *Jack Spratt* by Eileen Condon is inspired by this rhyme.

There Was an Old Woman Who Lived in a Shoe

There was an old woman who lived in a shoe.

She had so many children, she didn't know what to do;

She gave them some broth without any bread;

Then whipped them all soundly and put them to bed.

The nursery rhyme was first published in the 1790s. Its origins are uncertain.

Long ago, there was a custom of throwing a shoe after a bride as a blessing of fertility. The shoe may refer to this and the children to the success of the blessing. Another idea is that the shoe represents England and the children members of parliament.

The 'Old Woman' may refer to Queen Caroline, wife of George II, who had eight children; or to Elizabeth Vergoose of Boston who had six children and ten step-children.

Nora Farrell's story *There Was an Old Woman Who Lived in a Shoe* is inspired by this rhyme.

Rock a Bye Baby

Rock a Bye Baby on the tree top,

When the wind blows the cradle will rock,

When the bough breaks the cradle will fall,

And down will come baby, cradle and all.

The story of the nursery rhyme *Rock a Bye Baby* relates to a family who lived in a tree house which was formed within a yew tree. This yew tree was believed to be nearly 2000 years old. The family were charcoal burners who lived in Shining Cliff Woods, Ambergate, Derbyshire in the 1700s. Their names were Kate and Luke Kenyon and they lived in what was called the 'Betty Kenny Tree' – a colloquialism for Kate Kenyon. The Kenyons had eight children and a tree bough was hollowed out to act as a cradle for their children. Shining Cliff Woods was owned at the time by the Hurt family. The Kenyons were favoured by the Hurts who commissioned the artist James Ward of the Royal Academy to paint their portraits. The yew tree still exists but was severely fire-damaged by vandals in the 1930s.

The story *Rock a Bye Baby* by Majella Gorman is inspired by this rhyme.

The Spider and the Fly

'Will you walk into my parlour?' said the Spider to the Fly,

'Tis the prettiest little parlour that ever you did spy;

The way into my parlour is up a winding stair,

And I've a many curious things to show when you are there.'

'Oh no, no,' said the little Fly, 'to ask me is in vain,

For who goes up your winding stair

- can ne'er come down again.'

The Spider and the Fly is a poem by Mary Howitt (1799-1888), published in 1829. The opening line is one of the most recognized first lines in all of English verse. It is often used to indicate a false offer of help or friendship that is in fact a trap. The line has been used and parodied numerous times in various works of fiction.

The story *A Patch of Faded Blue* by Patrick Griffin is inspired by this rhyme.

Needles and Pins

Needles and pins,

Needles and pins,

When a man marries,

His trouble begins.

The origins of the rhyme are based on a traditional custom of husbands providing wives with money to purchase pins (as they were expensive at one time).

Sewing needles have been used since the Stone Age when they were made with bone, shells or thorns, various metals including iron, bronze, gold and silver. During the Middle Ages needle-making was quite an industry. Usually made from lengths of bronze wire, the eye of the needle was flattened on an anvil then a hole (eye) was driven through and finally the point of a needle was filed down. In London needle-makers formed themselves into a guild and worked near to the tailors who were based in Threeneedle (now Threadneedle) Street.

Pins followed a similar evolutionary path. There was a Guild of Pinmakers, or Pinners. Pins were relatively expensive during the Middle Ages and husbands gave their wives money especially for their purchase. As time went by pins became cheaper and the money could be spent on other items – hence the term 'pin money'.

The story *Needles and Pins* by Mary Healy is inspired by this rhyme.

Three Blind Mice

Three blind mice, three blind mice.

See how they run. See how they run.

They all ran after the farmer's wife

Who cut off their tails with a carving knife.

Did you ever see such a thing in your life

As three blind mice?

Before the Reformation Europe was Roman Catholic. After the reign of Henry VIII, England became largely Protestant. When Henry's daughter Mary became Queen she attempted, and failed, to return her people to Catholicism. She threatened the leaders of the English Reformation, the Archbishop of Canterbury Thomas Cranmer and Bishops Hugh Latimer and Nicholas Ridley, with execution if they did not recant. The 'Three Blind Mice' are said to represent these three men.

The story *Three Blind Men* by Orla Hennessy is based on historical fact but the characters Yon and Ellen are fictitious.

Humpty Dumpty

Humpty Dumpty sat on the wall,

Humpty Dumpty had a great fall,

All the King's horses,

All the King's men,

Couldn't put Humpty together again.

Humpty Dumpty was an unusually large cannon which was mounted on the protective wall of St Mary at the Walls Church in Colchester, England.

It was intended to protect the Parliamentarian stronghold of Colchester which was temporarily in control of the Royalists during the period of English history described as the English Civil War (1642-1649).

A shot from a Parliamentary cannon succeeded in damaging the wall underneath Humpty Dumpty causing the cannon to fall to the ground. The Royalists – 'all the King's men' – attempted to raise Humpty Dumpty onto another part of the wall but, even with the help of 'all the King's horses', failed in their task and Colchester fell to the Parliamentarians after a siege lasting eleven weeks.

Sir Charles Lucas and Lord Goring were both members of the Royalist Army. Lord Fairfax was a member of the Parliamentarian Army. All three men were active in leading attacks during the English Civil War including the siege at Colchester.

The story *The Fall of Many* by Stella Lanigan is inspired by this rhyme.

Twinkle, Twinkle, Little Star

Twinkle, twinkle, little star,
How I wonder what you are.
Up above the world so high,
Like a diamond in the sky.
Twinkle, twinkle, little star,
How I wonder what you are.

Jane Taylor was an English poet and novelist. She wrote the words for the song *Twinkle, Twinkle, Little Star*. The poem is now known worldwide, but its authorship is generally forgotten. It was first published under the title *The Star* in *Rhymes for the Nursery*, a collection of poems by Taylor and her older sister.

The story *Little Star* by Rachel Nolan is inspired by this rhyme.

Dr Foster

Dr Foster went to Gloucester

In a shower of rain.

He stepped in a puddle,

Right up to his middle,

And never went there again.

The point of departure for Valerie Ryan's story *Dr Foster's Patience Pays Off* is a 700-year-old folk rhyme from the Middle Ages. It tells of the fury and humiliation of England's proud Warrior King, Edward I, when he fell into a muddy stream on a visit to Gloucester and vowed never to return.

Author Biographies

R.A. Barnes

I've pedalled the pushbike of life until the chain fell off. Now living in rural Ireland where the natives are friendly and the weather atrocious, I write crime fiction and thrillers with four published novels to date (*Peril, The Baptist, Getting Out of Dodge* and *Koobi Fora*). I also have stories published in three other anthologies – *Original Sins, Knife Edge* and *Edge of Passion*.

My writing is dedicated to the memory of my late Scottish grandfather Robert 'Ruby' Aloysius Barnes.

Contact ruby.barnes@marblecitypublishing.com

www.rubybarnes.blogspot.com

Maura Barrett

Maura is indeed a Writer and a Librarian but that is where the comparisons to her story end. She grew up in the Comeragh Mountains and lives now beneath Sliabhnamon. Maura says that there is a language in landscape that fires her imagination. It is sprinkled with metaphor. The ordinary everyday event seeps out of the subconscious and tells the deeper story.

www.simplesite.com/her-story

Jeanne Beary

Jeanne is a Kildare-based writer. Her writings have been published, recorded and broadcast. Her work has been shortlisted for the Francis MacManus competition, received first place in *Stellar* magazine's Write On competition and been included in a number of short story collections.

Ilona Blunden

Ilona won the Cecil Day Lewis Poetry Award and was shortlisted for the RTÉ Radio 1 Francis MacManus Short Story Competition. Ilona's story *Wonderland* appeared in *Original Sins*, an anthology of new Irish writing. Her story *The Anniversary* appeared on *Stories for the Ear (vol. 2)*, broadcast by the Kildare Arts Service.

Phyllida Clarke

Mother, grandmother, writer, artist, university lecturer and practising mediator. It is better to be lucky than rich. I find four-leafed clovers when I need them.

Eileen Condon

Eileen is a native New Yorker, living in the Knockmealdown Mountains. Her stories have appeared in the following anthologies: Original Sins, Knife Edge and Edge of Passion. Another story, Stronger Than Any Flower, was dramatized into a radio play for KCLR and performed in Bewley's Theatre on Grafton St, Dublin. She was also long-listed for the Fish Short Story Competition.

Eileen's short memory piece was chosen for the Spring 2015 edition of *Northwest Words*, an on-line literary journal. She would like to learn how to reverse a trailer into a yard without knocking the piers.

Nora Farrell

A heron visits the river near her home. She has tried to stare at him longer than he stares at the swirling water but Nora has never succeeded at this endeavour. She loves sunrise, birdsong and *Swan Lake*. She writes for fun.

Majella Gorman

Majella is a Tipperary-based writer. She lives in Thurles with her husband John and two children. She blogs at www.majellagormanwrites.blogspot.ie

Patrick Griffin

Patrick is from Kilkenny and is currently studying for a Masters in Creative Writing at UL. He has been a Francis MacManus short story winner, broadcast on RTE. His work was also performed at the Frank O'Connor Short Story Festival. One of his plays was performed in Bewley's Theatre, Dublin. A number of his stories have been anthologized.

Mary Healy

Mary is a first-class honours graduate of NUI Maynooth Creative Writing for Publication. Her work has been published in several anthologies and features on the RTE

Ten and Stinging Fly websites and has been broadcast on radio. She has also won prizes in The Irish Writers' Centre and features in their archives.

In 2012, Mary won the UCD Masters Anthology Competition and is published in their collection of short stories *New Tricks with Matches*. In 2012, she was also highly commended on the shortlist in the Bryan MacMahon Short Story Competition in Listowel Writers' week. Another short story reached the top ten of the RTE Guide / Penguin Ireland Short Story Competition.

In June 2014, one of Mary's stories was published in the Cork County Library Winners' Anthology. Mary was also recently shortlisted in the Fish Flash Fiction Competition.

Mary blogs at www.maryhealybooks.blogspot.com

Orla Hennessy

Orla lives in Kilkenny. She has completed three years of Creative Writing for Publication with NUIM and has stories published in the anthology Original Sins.

Her first novel The Left House has been long-listed for the Irish Writers Centre Novel Fair 2015.

Stella Lanigan

Born and bred in County Tipperary where I now live. Between raising a family and working part-time, free time is infrequent. The creative writing course in St Kieran's, Kilkenny encouraged me to find my own voice and be a master of many words when it came to the blank page. I'll be forever grateful.

Rachel Nolan

I have loved stories ever since Lucy found the wardrobe and I've been looking for adventure in the pages of books ever since.

I am working on my first novel while doing my M. Phil. in Intercultural Theology and Interreligious Studies at the ISE in Trinity College Dublin with the hopes of changing the world. My favourite things are a mug of tea made by somebody else and squeezy hugs.

Valerie Ryan

Valerie's stories have been shortlisted for a number of awards and broadcast on radio. She is the author of *The Story of Russborough House* which tells of the lives of the owners of the West Wicklow stately home over three centuries. She works as a journalist and teaches in adult education.

Connect with Marble City Publishing

http://www.marblecitypublishing.com

Join Marble City's list for updates on new releases, special
offers and competitions:

http://eepurl.com/vek5L

Follow on Twitter:
http://twitter.com/MarbleCityPub

An anthology of twenty-five crime, thriller, mystery and suspense stories from twenty-three authors, including Booker prize nominated Jim Williams. All profits to Booktrust.org.uk

This global collection of short stories from 500 to 4000 words covers everything from cosy mystery to urban noir, gumshoe and classic crime.

An anthology of twenty-one crime, mystery, suspense and romance stories from nineteen authors, including Emmy-nominated John Goldsmith and Booker-nominated Jim Williams.

This global collection of short stories from 400 to 7000 words covers everything from crime fiction to romantic suspense and historical mystery.

Twelve Curious Deaths In France

John Goldsmith

A collection of stories by international bestselling author and Emmy-nominated screenwriter John Goldsmith.

Do miracles really happen? Did Voltaire rise from the dead? Is our fate predestined? Are sex toys dangerous? The answers are to be found in this remarkable collection. Includes how-to advice on a number of topics: delivering practical jokes from beyond the grave; how best to murder an African despot; the secret of the world's best rabbit stew. From fantastic to factual, contemporary to historical, a mix of comedy, drama, intrigue and suspense.

The teenage John Baptist murdered his brother in a bathtub. Condemned to a secure mental institution, he met Mary and they bonded. But young and crazy love rarely endures. Electrotherapy wiped John's memory and he was cured.

Twenty years later, John has become a respectable, slightly overweight and balding pillar of society with a wife and young family. Then he starts to remember...

Told from a serial killer's viewpoint and combining elements of Criminal Minds and Dexter, The Baptist is a deceptive view of normality through the lens of a man obsessed by religious mania and a woman driven insane by lust.

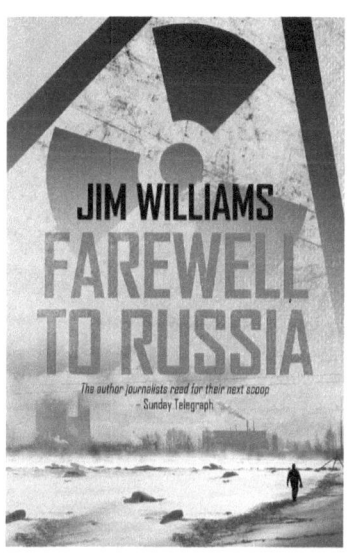

JIM WILLIAMS

FAREWELL TO RUSSIA

The author journalists read for their next scoop
– Sunday Telegraph

The unthinkable has happened at the Soviet nuclear plant at Sokolskoye. An accident of such terrifying proportions, of such catastrophic ecological and political consequence that a curtain of silence is drawn ominously over the incident. Major Pyotr Kirov of the KGB is appointed to extract the truth from the treacherous minefield of misinformation and intrigue and to obtain from the West the technology essential to prevent further damage. But the vital equipment is under strict trade embargo...

And in London, George Twist, head of a company which manufactures the technology, is on the verge of bankruptcy and desperate to win the illegal contract. Can he deliver on time? Will he survive a frantic smuggling operation across the frozen wastes of Finland? Can he wrong-foot the authorities ... and his own conscience? Is it possible to say farewell to Russia?